COLLISION COURSE!

Sturgis saw the Russian copter turn and come at his own copter, guns blazing.

"Track!" he commanded his suit-computer, but the readout in his helmet was dim and blurry, barely readable. The battery that powered his suit was damaged. Suddenly he noticed that the joints of his suit were stiffening. He didn't have much longer before he froze completely. Damn!

Sturgis turned his copter into the path of the oncoming White Wolf and girded himself for a head-on midair collision. There were worse ways to die.

"It's either you or me," he said softly. "Maybe it's gonna be both of us."

DOOMSDAY WARRIOR
by Ryder Stacy

After the nuclear devastation of World War III, America is no more than a brutalized colony of the Soviet master. But only until Ted Rockson, soldier of survival, leads a rebellion against the hated conquerers . . .

DOOMSDAY WARRIOR	(1356, $2.95)
#2: RED AMERICA	(1419, $2.50)
#5: AMERICA'S LAST DECLARATION	(1608, $2.50)
#6: AMERICAN REBELLION	(1659, $2.50)
#7: AMERICAN DEFIANCE	(1745, $2.50)
#8: AMERICAN GLORY	(1812, $2.50)
#9: AMERICA'S ZERO HOUR	(1929, $2.50)

Available wherever paperbacks are sold, or order direct from the Publisher. Send cover price plus 50¢ per copy for mailing and handling to Zebra Books, Dept. 1893, 475 Park Avenue South, New York, N.Y. 10016. Residents of New York, New Jersey and Pennsylvania must include sales tax. DO NOT SEND CASH.

C.A.D.S.

#3 TECH COMMANDO

BY JOHN SIEVERT

ZEBRA BOOKS
KENSINGTON PUBLISHING CORP.

ZEBRA BOOKS

are published by

Kensington Publishing Corp.
475 Park Avenue South
New York, NY 10016

Copyright © 1986 by John Sievert

All rights reserved. No part of this book may be reproduced in any form or by any means without the prior written consent of the Publisher, excepting brief quotes used in reviews.

First printing: September 1986

Printed in the United States of America

PROLOGUE

THE C.A.D.S. FORCE – A secret American combined-services unit of high-tech commandos trained for penetrating radioactive enemy-held areas. Each Tech Commando, or *Blacksuit,* as the Soviet enemy calls them, wears the most advanced combat armor suit the world has ever known. The C.A.D.S. suit (COMPUTERIZED ATTACK/DEFENSE SYSTEM) is seven feet high, made of stress-plastic and alloy steel. It is equipped with a variety of built-in weapons systems, each capable of awesome destruction. The computerized visionscreen/visor of the helmet has a dozen sensor modes, each far beyond normal human abilities.

The C.A.D.S. suit makes any man that wears it nearly invincible. In the suit, a man has the power of a god of old.

After a surprise nuclear attack on Christmas Eve, 1997, the Soviets landed an invasion force onto the east coast of the ravaged U.S. Only the C.A.D.S. unit, led by Colonel Dean Sturgis, aka The Tech Commando, had the power to oppose them. Sturgis, an American officer of uncanny physical abilities, tactical knowledge, and courage, led the C.A.D.S. Force into battle against the invaders. For the time being, C.A.D.S. must go it alone—for the country is in shambles, all civilian and military authority collapsed.

Half the population died from radiation, plague, and starvation within the first month. Countless millions now wander through the rubble in a zombielike daze. Society has quickly reverted to a primitive state where dog-eat-dog is the new morality. Bandit gangs have sprung up everywhere, ruling their little kingdoms with iron fists. Those who possess weapons live—those who don't, die. A few traitorous nuke survivors—motorcycle gangs, other lawless elements of the old U.S.A.—have thrown in their lot with the Soviets.

In the east, much is radioactive wasteland—a mosaic of safe and unsafe areas. New wind patterns are making parts of the Appalachian Mountains and bits of the southlands relatively habitable. In the west, nuke-spawned earthquakes ravage the land. Locusts and raven flocks blacken the skies attacking the weak, the wounded. The nuke survivors battle it out for the few remaining supplies.

From the new wartime capital located in the secret underground base at White Sands, New Mexico, President Williamson takes steps to reach out to restore the basic functions of U.S. society. White Sands is establishing scrambled radio contact with the viable U.S. military posts throughout the land. By using Vietnam vets as organizers and sending them throughout the land, the President hopes to establish "fortified hamlets" that will greet the Russians with hellfire at every step of their march westward, when it comes.

But the President needs time to accomplish these goals. The C.A.D.S. Commandos are the means of buying that time—with blood. The high-tech strike force of "Blacksuits," under Colonel Dean Sturgis, rescued the President from a bombed-out and occupied Washington, D.C. and brought him safely to White Sands. (*C.A.D.S. #1*) Then the C.A.D.S. unit destroyed the Soviet harbor and fleet at Charleston with a daring—and costly—raid. The C.A.D.S. unit must stay in the east—where the battle is being fought. They have set up a base deep within Georgia's Okefenokee Swamp. There Colonel Dean Sturgis and his men plan more devastating raids against the Soviets. But they are desperately short of supplies. And every day more Soviet troops and supplies land all along the eastern seaboard!

CHAPTER ONE

A strange seven-foot-tall black-metal figure stood at the top of a barren Georgia hillside, staring into the distance with what appeared to be one giant mirrorlike eye. Inside the black armor suit that looked like an invader from Mars was Colonel Dean Sturgis, leader of the C.A.D.S. Force.

The C.A.D.S. suit made Sturgis and his Tech Commandos the last hope of the nuke-war-ravaged U.S. The battle-armor suit was America's high-tech miracle, a near-impervious killing machine of plastic and steel armed with powerful weapons unmatched even on a modern tank. But it was only as good as the man in it. Guts and skill and iron nerve meshed with machine.

Colonel Sturgis was sealed in a temperature- and rad-proof environment, his every movement assisted, amplified, by servo-mechanism drives. Though the suit weighed four hundred and fifty pounds, Sturgis moved like an impossibly tireless Olympic athlete.

The colonel had been traveling north for two days now. He was in the western wilderness area of Georgia. Silhouetted by the rising orange sun, the Tech

Commando stood among the twisted and burned tree trunks and surveyed the countryside with granular brown eyes. Nothing alive. Just charred forest ahead.

Inside the mirrorlike visorscreen, fatigue etched the lines on the brow beneath touseled, sweat-matted dusty blond hair. This "short time frame" search for Robin had become a nightmare. Any other man would have turned back.

"Read out altitude and rad level," he commanded. Immediately his voice-activated suit-computer sent a stream of red digital letters across the bottom of his visor screen.

ALTITUDE—2340 FEET. RAD LEVEL 3.2/HR. UNINHABITABLE AREA. ACCEPTABLE LEVEL FOR PASSAGE.

Radiation. No wonder the terrain looked as dead as a lunar landscape, though this was spring, late March. The sun faded behind a dark-gray fallout cloud. Oh, what has man done to the world, Sturgis thought.

Sturgis had traveled from his base in the Okefenokee Swamp at high speed toward a rendezvous with Robin, his wife, leaving his trusted friend, Lt. Tranh Van Noc, in charge. He had circled wide around what was left of Atlanta after a nuke-spawned fire.

He had been *too anxious* to reach Robin.

The tribike, a three-barrel-wheeled motorcycle with an atomic fuel-cell, had made speed too tempting. On the sleek low-slung bike, Sturgis roared up Route 61 at one hundred plus miles per hour. There had been a trap—a false bit of roadway. A deep pit with sharpened steel beams deep down inside it. Were it not for the armor of his suit, he would not have survived. His space-age motorcycle had been wrecked beyond repair.

When Sturgis crawled up out of the pit, he found deep gouges carved across his breastplate. Half the suit's sensors had been damaged.

The Revengers, freedom fighters who controlled most of Georgia, had probably laid the trap. If so, they had nearly killed their most valuable friend.

And so here he was on this barren hill, after walking the last twenty-one miles. His suit's power pack was down to ten percent of capacity. He had no idea how he'd get it back. But getting back was for later. Right now the objective, the only objective, was to push onward.

"Computer replot direction of Stone Mountain Monument Park," he intoned with dry lips. Immediately the screen indicated BEARING 34. He turned his head toward the distant hump of mountains and sighed. "How far?"

DISTANCE 49 KILOMETERS.

Out there was Robin, the woman he loved, his reason for living—the love he hadn't seen since before the surprise nuke strike on Christmas Eve, three long, hard months ago. At almost every moment he had not been engaged in life-or-death battle during those months, he had been thinking of Robin. Of her long, flowing brown hair, her warmth, her embraces. With her, life had a feeling just the opposite of the one this cruel, twisted world before him conjured up:

Love, not hate. Life, not death . . .

Snapping out of his reverie of Robin, Sturgis commanded, "Macro view." The image displayed before him on the computerized visor changed from a normal view of the fire-ravaged countryside to an enhanced blue-tinted depiction of a five-mile area. Any humans or any metallic objects would be pin-pointed by this vision mode of the high-tech suit's computer. But no telltale blinking red dots appeared. Still, there was all sorts of interference like snow on a TV receiver, due to the damage incurred in the metal-spike pit—or perhaps from the radiation interference. The suit's sensors functioned partially by bouncing electromagnetic force beams, sent from its bristling stubby antennas, off the low layers of air.

Sturgis sighed. He felt so alone. Only the suit was his companion on this journey. A coffinlike presence, and a friend.

He ordered, "Clear screen." The view became clear again; he saw the world before him with human eyes. "Telescopic mode, bearing thirty-four degrees," he intoned. The zoom view of a distant ripple on the mountain became a bald-faced hill. "Infra-enhance." It became less blurred. Yes, that was the mountain at the beginning of the range that Sturgis was searching for. He was sure of it. "Match line-of-sight and grid map of Georgia. Project name of object."

The computer readout said MT. REDFACE. ELEVATION 3210. That was it. That meant he had less than fifty miles to go. Robin's note to him, the note he had found in their farm-fortress in Virginia, had given him the time and place to meet her. He could recite the note from memory:

Darling: There are two groups of attackers outside fighting for the privilege of having me—I'm taking the opportunity to slip away. If you find this note, I'm going to the place we camped on our honeymoon. Remember?

Love, Robin

If Robin had been smart, she had kept away from the burned-out radioactive cities, away from the stalled cars full of decaying bodies on the interstates. He hoped she had, and that she was just fifty miles away. But there were crazed gangs of survivors out there, and Soviet patrols, and a million other dangers. No time to waste. Sturgis hurried down the hill in bounding strides.

Viking stared through his grimy Zeiss 7x50 binoculars with rapt interest. *There!*—a strange metal-suited figure running down the bare hill to the southeast.

"Okay, you fuckers," Viking yelled, turning his semidissolved, pus-dripping twisted face to them. His wild red-eyed stare shot fear into all who were on its receiving end.

"Get your dirt bikes into the fucking woods, lay them down. Someone's comin'."

The dozen biker terrorists with hammer-and-sickle emblems newly painted on the backs of their black leather jackets moved rapidly to obey. They always obeyed their horn-helmeted leader. He was dangerous, totally mad, but he was their meal ticket in a country that each day had less and less food.

Viking smiled. He took up the binoculars again and looked up. The robot-man was still coming and he apparently hadn't seen anything, for he headed their way with long, loping strides.

Viking had only seen one of this kind before. Two

months earlier, he and his first gang of riders had been besieging a bomb shelter in Virginia. A similar black-metal figure had come upon them riding a weird three-wheeled motorcycle. The Blacksuit—that's what the Reds called them—had killed all of his gang except Bug and Stan and him. The three had hid, bleeding and frightened, in the woods for days, until they were sure he was gone. And then they had gone to the deserted shelter and found all they needed: Food, medicines, bandages, pure water. Afraid the Blacksuit would return, they had taken to the road again. They had gotten the drop on some other marauding bikers; Viking had killed their leader and assumed his place. The new gang had grown to twelve. Then the Reds had caught them. And Viking had struck the deal with Bukarov: He had become a turncoat. Why the hell not, he thought. He had always hated the authorities. The cops, the judges, the prison guards. The Reds had all the cards now. They had the *power.*

The figure was less than sixty yards away. "Bug, get your fucking bazooka up—we're gonna get him. Bukarov told me that if we bring back one of these Blacksuit guys, even if he's in pieces, we'll all be given anything we want. The rest of you," Viking snarled, "get your rifles up." They all crouched low along the treeline, just out of sight of the figure in the field.

"Should we load?" whispered Bug.

"Of course, you idiot," Viking whispered. "Let him get a bit closer, then blast him."

Bug smiled his toothless grin. "Yeah. Okay." He lifted the long brown-painted tube onto his shoulder, lined the approaching metal-man in the sight. Weasel, crouching down behind him, slid the long projectile into the breech and clicked it shut.

Luckily for Sturgis he had the Ampli mode up high. He heard the whispers from the treeline, and the computer pinpointed the source near the big elm tree. He stopped in his tracks for an instant. He was out in the open fifty yards from the source of the sounds. "G.I. mode," he ordered. The suit's visor displayed now what the sensors had missed earlier. TWELVE MEN, A K-2 CZECH BAZOOKA. MANY SMALL ARMS. TEN TO TWELVE METAL OBJECTS, POSSIBLY MOTORCYCLES. Sturgis smiled. Reds? He was about to launch an E-ball at the hidden source of the whispers, then he hesitated. The whispers had been in English. Not Russian. Maybe those hiding there were freedom fighters, with a *captured* Czech bazooka. He held his fire. Sturgis decided to get closer to cover, however. A direct bazooka hit could be fatal, even in the C.A.D.S. armor.

He cut diagonally toward a fallen tree. When he was ten feet from it, he turned up his Address mode and shouted, "You there in hiding, identify yourselves. I'm an American." His voice boomed through the hills.

"Fire," Viking yelled. Bug did as ordered. The rocket leapt from the bazooka and headed toward Sturgis at tremendous velocity. But the automatic emergency jet system of his backpack hurled the Tech Commando into the air just in time for the shell to flash past his steel boots. The rifle fire from the ten Kalashnikovs had no effect, the few shots hitting his armor ricocheting harmlessly from it.

Sturgis cut the jets and fell behind the tree stump,

easily taking the crushing force of the landing with the servomechanism compensators built into the suit. He crouched there and leaned his arm-weapons tube over the bare crumbling wood. "Fire E-ball at target." Sturgis felt a jerk and heard the clunk of the loading mechanism. The E-ball, a tremendous electrically charged hot projectile flamed from the tube straight toward the treeline.

The huge old elm was smashed to pieces, two human figures were blown into the air like torn rag dolls. A long tube—the bazooka—sailed over the trees, still smoking.

Sturgis heard a gruff voice yell "Spread out, assholes," and he smiled. It wouldn't do them any good. Their only ace, the bazooka, was out of action.

The Red-mode helmet readout told the story: Only eight of them still alive. He stood erect, walked around the stump and toward the woods, his right arm extended. He heard the start-up roar of many motorcycles. "Jet, fifty feet high, forward, sixty degree climb," he ordered. The suit rose on the blue flame of its jetpack and Sturgis soared up over the small trees. In a few seconds he traveled a thousand yards, and came down on the thick, trunklike branch of an old gnarled oak. He cut the jets when he found the branch would support his suit's heavy weight, and stood and waited.

In a few seconds two bikers riding parallel tore up the pine-needle floor of the forest directly under him. Sturgis leapt down on them, letting the crushing steel cleats of his boots hit directly on a shoulder of each of the men. They fell writhing as their bikes spun out from under them. One was trying to get up; the other didn't move but lay there in an impossible position, his neck broken. Sturgis noticed the hammer-and-sickle emblem on the back of the other's jacket as, somehow, he rose and tried to stagger off. He let him have a taste of liquid-plastic fire. The LPF flames shot forth with such intensity that in the second before Sturgis cut the flow, the man was nothing but a charred cinder.

Sturgis turned as another cycle bored directly down on him. The startled rider, a bearded man with a coonskin cap, managed to get off a few shots with his Tokarov pistol. Sturgis turned his right arm slightly and intoned, "SMG—twelve rounds." The man fell under the withering burst of 9mm explosive bullets, the bike flying by the right of the black nightmare figure that was called the Tech Commando.

The next two riders took one look at the monster standing over the crumpled and smoking bodies and turned their bikes, kicking up dirt. But they were Red pawns, traitors. They had to be *destroyed*, Sturgis resolved.

"LPF again!" Sturgis commanded, lifting his right arm and firing flaming death out of the tube. The bikers ignited and they drove away as human torches, looking like burning pinwheels in the wind. Sturgis heard more cycles off to his right. He hit Jump mode, took off in that direction, eager for another fight. And he found it!

There was the one in the viking helmet, with three of his buddies—Sturgis landed well ahead of them and he waited. Sturgis clearly heard the cursing, frightened voices of the two bikers tearing up the rotted leaves and roots on his Ampli mode, the sound of the dirt bikes' roar screened out by the computer.

"Let's get the fuck out of here, Viking. The guy can't be hurt. He's like—"

"No," the gruff voice cut the frightened one off, "we aren't leaving, we're staying here in these woods and getting him. When we get him, we'll be rich." Viking was sure he'd kill the Blacksuit. He had a special modification to his 1300 cc Kawasaki cycle that would do the job. He just needed the *chance*.

They were upon him. Sturgis just stood in the way, a steel wall of death. My god, the colonel thought, seeing the half-dissolved, bulging-eyed face under the twin-horned viking helmet—I think I've seen this character before!

The bikes skidded to a halt, and as Viking put out a foot to steady his bike, he squeezed a hidden trigger near the clutch mechanism on the handlebar. Too late Sturgis saw the 105mm barrel of an RPG launcher jutting over the helmeted rider's front fender. An armor-piercing shell hurtled directly at him. The automatic mechanisms of the suit tried to get Sturgis out of the way, but he didn't make it.

The special dual-flange-headed Soviet projectile smashed a hole in the right lower side of his C.A.D.S. suit's torso. Sturgis collapsed in tremendous pain, his systems overload and malfunction indicators buzzing wildly in his helmet. His visor clouded over for a second and then went to clear. The colonel rolled over and brought up his right-arm tube and fired submachine-gun tracers at the pair. But only the helmetless rider was hit, the other was nowhere to be seen. There was smoke!

The impact of the cyclist's projectile caused a fire

in the Tech Commando's suit's electrical system. There was only one thing to do. Get out fast. But bullets were zinging at him from behind a large boulder. He might be dead without his suit, but he'd surely die with it on. He'd be fried.

Sturgis saw the blinking SERIOUS MALFUNCTION readout flash on his screen. Then the dreaded EXPLOSION COUNTDOWN FROM SEVENTY SECONDS, meaning the power pack had gone critical, flashed—and Sturgis had to get out of the suit fast. The readout was blinking off the seconds he had left—52, 51, 50, 49 . . .—it normally took at least a minute to get out of the suit. He blew the leg- and arm-gauntlet bolts. All the while Viking was rushing away. But when he heard the steel-plastic bolts pop, he turned to see Sturgis's helmet come off—and he leered with anticipation.

Viking steadied his Kalashnikov submachine gun on the rock and lined it up on the man. He'd wait until his armor was off, and then he'd tease the man a little, shoot at his heels, make him dance for a while. Then Viking would finish him off.

Grimacing in pain, Sturgis continued to grunt out the dissassembly-unlock sequence code. Bolts of steel opened, the torso part of his near-invincible outfit separated along invisible seams. Other electrically sealed hinges and bolts started blowing open. He had no choice. He was bleeding badly—there were pieces of shrapnel in his gut too. Sturgis freed himself from the last section of his suit.

Laughter. "Hey, spaceman, what's the matter, getting all burned up?" yelled the man behind the boulder, pouring a burst of automatic fire from his place of concealment. Sturgis dove behind a thick tree. The abrupt movement sent racking pain through his guts. All Sturgis now had to defend himself was the service .45 on his waist. A pistol against submachine guns.

More bullets chipped away at the ground around the tree. Some were coming from another direction—damn, there were more of them now—coming like hyenas to take down the wounded prey. But Sturgis vowed he would not die until they were all dead—should be seven of them. He realized the power pack of the C.A.D.S. suit hadn't blown yet. But he could hear the high-pitched humming sound of the overload. It *would* explode soon! Sturgis rolled and crawled and rolled again away from the C.A.D.S. suit. When it blew, it would take anyone within twenty feet of it with it in a shrapnel-filled explosion. He managed to get new cover behind a fallen tree.

"He's out of his suit," snarled the leader of the traitor pack. "Get it!—You, Weasel; Mikey—Go over there and get it."

Sturgis smiled. He wished the hell they would *all* try to get it. He pressed his hand against his wound—without the suit he would have been blown into a million pieces. The direct hit had bloodied him and there were sharp pieces of metal in his skin, but the bleeding wasn't profuse. It hurt, especially when he had crawled to this cover, but he was alive—and he could fight. He smiled and unholstered the .45 that C.A.D.S. Commandos always had strapped around the waist of their black coveralls inside their suits—it was a regulation that seemed useless most of the time. Now Sturgis was glad he had routinely gone by the book the last time he suited up. He had an extra magazine of fifteen also. But he didn't waste a shot on the two crouch-running figures that made for the suit. He just waited.

"Hey, Viking, we got it," a voice yelled. "It's smoking but—" There was a tremendous explosion and parts of the men that had just reached the suit flew up in the air along with a mushrooming orange ball. Low-hanging branches were set afire; pieces of shattered bone and metal stuck in the tree trunks for fifty feet.

He heard motorcycles start up, roaring into life. But they weren't getting closer. They were receding. The rest of the traitors were abandoning the fight, scrambling away in real terror. They must have thought I had a bunch of grenades!

He stood up and fired a burst after them but they were already shielded by the trees. He wanted to chase them but it hurt too much. When Sturgis reached the field's edge he saw five cyclists, including the leader, riding up a hill—far out of range of his .45. Sturgis reholstered the weapon and sat down on the ground. He tore open his coveralls with the utility knife on his belt and took a strip of gauze from the medipac and dabbed it over the wound. Wiping the blood away, he saw a series of inch-wide slashes oozing red. But the bleeding was stopping. Two of the small wounds displayed some shiny jagged fragments of metal jutting from them. He pulled them out, wincing in pain when he did so. Then he taped the wounds up with the antiseptic-impregnated adhesive bandages in his kit. He had to get out of the area, he realized. Some of those guys had rifles. If they realized he only had a

.45, they would get just out of range and then snipe and snipe at him until he was hit. No, he had to make himself scarce. Sturgis went back into the woods and headed north. Guided by his hand-held compass, he still could make it by nightfall. Robin. Find Robin.

"Motherfucker!" Viking said, and slammed his leather-gloved hand across the cheek of Squat, the shortest of his gang. The missing-toothed gnomelike man in his forties, the shine of his bald pate covered by soot and grease, cringed.

"I didn't do nothin'," Squat said, sitting up from his fall and wiping his face. "Honest, I—"

"Oh, shut up," Viking said disgustedly. They were gathered around a small campfire a mile from the aborted fight. Viking was surly, grumbling. He wasn't feeling too good about losing his prize. When the robot suit had blown up, he figured there was no sense staying around to see what other tricks the sandy-haired guy had in store. He had missed his big chance of impressing his employers, missed being a *big man*. "Shit."

Nervously pulling on his long tousled gray hair, Knuck, the oldest member of Viking's gang, asked, "Shouldn't we report finding the Blacksuit guy to the Sovs, boss?"

Viking snapped back gruffly. "Are you that stupid, shitface? If we told them that we let him get away, that he destroyed the suit—and that we let him—we'd all be pushing up daisies. You let *me* do the thinking around here. We don't have to tell the Reds everything. You've got food—right? And guns? And women—when we find them? Right? And that's thanks to *me*, Viking." He poked his chest with a forefinger. "Right?"

The gang murmured approval, nodded.

"Well, then *I* do the thinking. Understand?" His wild eyes took in every one of the five.

"Yeah, sure, right," they said in a mixed chorus.

"Good. Now—Knuck. You pull out that Exxon map of Georgia. What's the next town we gotta liberate? Oh yeah, Carollton. How many miles from here?"

"About twenty, boss," Knuck said, after studying the torn and dirty roadmap.

"Well, what are we waiting for? Let's go."

CHAPTER TWO

His lips cracked from thirst, his wounded side throbbing, Sturgis reached the area of the Stone Mountain Monument Park. Without the sophisticated guidance equipment of the C.A.D.S. suit, he had been going by dead reckoning and the little pocket compass. He'd made good time, considering.

It was still light. Sturgis was sure that he hadn't been followed. Several times along the way Sturgis had had a clear view for miles behind him from a hilltop. He was sure he hadn't been pursued. He'd never want to lead an enemy to Robin.

The sun was setting now, shafts of orange light arching up through dark clouds—the dark clouds that almost always had shrouded the sky since the nuke attack. Unlike the Okefenokee area, this part of the South showed little signs of spring. But Sturgis had seen a few tracks—rabbits, deer—along the last part of his trek. And the trees in this area weren't burned.

He came out of the woods and onto a dirt road. He walked north on the road. This looked familiar. His heart pounded with excitement when he saw the old weathered sign on the post: SMOKY MOUNTAIN—The rest of the sign had split off and fallen. He walked around the chains drawn across the road—the park had been closed for the winter—probably would never greet tourists and campers again. He walked for another ten minutes, looking for the poorly marked rugged trail to the remote campsite. He found the tall clump of ponderosa pines that were the indicators of the way. There! A path. He turned off the road and began the steep hike.

He was deep in the evergreens now, and whether it was the crisp mountain air, or the thought of being so close to his goal, Sturgis didn't know—but he felt better, almost exhilarated. He found the little babbling brook and its rough-hewn wood bridge. He immediately bent by the brook and, cupping his hands for a vessel, drank thirstily for a long time. Then he moved on. Yards now.

He came to the little rock-strewn clearing. He saw the tall stately elm tree where he and Robin had carved their initials eight years and three days earlier. But it was broken in half, many of its branches fallen to the ground. It looked like it might have been hit by lightning. There were holes in it, rotted wood. There was no one here!

Stepping over a large twisted branch, he walked up to the tree trunk and sat down with his back against it, determined to wait for Robin if it took forever. He faced the last traces of light in the west. The hills in the distance had become a dark ochre color. Blood. He watched the sky for a long time, watched the first stars come out. He was so still that eventually a doe and a fawn appeared at the edge of the clearing and came out to nibble on some tender young shoots in the clearing, not fifteen yards away. The animals brought Sturgis out of his feeling of utter loneliness. Finally, he coughed once. The doe and fawn, startled, raised their heads. Their big white ears twitched into the wind. They sniffed. As he arose, they took off, leaping gracefully back amongst the bushes.

Abandoning all caution, Sturgis called out, "Robin, it's me, Dean. I'm here. Where are you?" He took out the tiny chemical flashlight from his utility belt and he walked quickly around the clearing—looking for any signs that someone had been there. He was about to give up when on the eastern edge of the clearing he found the marks made by the stakes for a small tent. And he found a set of stones arranged in a circle, with burnt charcoal and pieces of wood in the center. He lifted a charred stick and examined it in the light beam. He rubbed the burnt end with his hand, and soot came off. The fire had been made in the last few days.

He lifted each rock in turn looking for a note—anything. And then he thought, *No, the tree!*

Sturgis ran like a wild man, leapt over the fallen branch, and ran around the tree playing the light over the gnarled bark . . . *There.* The heart with the inscription *"Dean and Robin 4ever".*

They had carved that there on their honeymoon. There was a big hole in the tree where a branch had broken off long ago, and the glint of something in the hollow.

He reached in and dug out some leaves and found a jar—the kind country folk use for canning. And there was a note inside. He opened the jar, extracted the note and read it, his hand shaking so much he could hardly see the words.

Dear Dean,

I'm writing this March 28, 1998. I've been here three days now. I can't stay any longer. So I'm leaving this note. I am safe and staying with some wonderful American patriots—Jeb and his wife Sally, and Hiram and Babs, and Al Gastin, and lots of others. They fight the Russians at every turn. I have a young companion, Chris, a boy age 12. He helped me make it to Georgia. I am safe and happy and as well as I can be under the circumstances. Not knowing if you are alive or dead is a pain in my heart. I can't tell you where I am in case some enemy finds this note—please leave a message here for me—deeper in the hole in the tree. The only thing I can think to say that an enemy couldn't use is meet me on your birthday—right here at noon. I don't think anyone's been here since the nukes fell—come to me next time. Please, Dean, leave a note if you can. I will check this tree again before then. I hope to find your note here—but whether I do or not I will be here on your birthday. With love forever, *your wife, Robin.*

Sturgis's heart felt like a limp sponge. *One day ago* she had been here, alive, safe. He took out a small pad and attached magnetic pen, wrote a reply:

Dearest Robin, my wife, I just missed you by a day. I am well, fighting with a special unit of commandos against the Soviets. Take heart, we will win. I will come back here if I can on the date of my birthday. Love, Dean.

She had left another gift—a can of Spam. He opened it and ate it with immense gratitude. After putting his note in the jar, and back in the tree-hole, he fell asleep against the gnarled trunk.

In the morning at first light, he headed west toward I-51. Sturgis had an idea. A wild idea.

When he reached the interstate, he searched among the abandoned cars there for one with a stickshift. He found an old VW Beetle. Of course, it had sat there all winter, abandoned, most likely, in the immense traffic jam of N-Day. The key was in the ignition. He didn't try to start it, not just yet. He checked the battery. It had water in it and the cables weren't corroded. The wiring looked okay. He decided to try his idea—try jump-starting it. Pushing against the open driver-side door, with the car in neutral, he moved it down the gently sloping road till he could barely keep up. Then he jumped in, depressed the clutch, and shifted into first. He pumped the gas and let the clutch up. The third time he did this, the car actually started.

Sturgis, elated, roared the engine for five minutes and only then looked at the gas meter—*half full*! This area had been far enough from the EMP* of the nukes to save the electrical system. A roll-start was all it needed. He patted the dashboard. "Good old boy." He tried the radio—nothing but static. Then, faintly, a voice! "And so the Soviet Provisional Government proudly announces the following benefits for those Americans who wish to take advantage of the general amnesty for counter-revolutionary elements in the Eastern Occupation Zone! One—no reprisals against you or your family; two—food for one month, during which you will be reeducated into the values of Marxism-Leninism; three— . . ." The signal faded.

Sturgis smiled. Such an offer meant the Reds were hurting. the Revengers were doing a *job* with their old hunting rifles and Molotov cocktails. America

*Electromagnetic pulse—an energy that destroys electrical equipment.

was down, but not out.

He floored the little vehicle and, whistling, "America the Beautiful," sped down the interstate. All the traffic had been on the side of the road heading away from Atlanta, so once he pushed a few cars out of the way, and bumped the VW over a divider, he had the whole road to himself, open and unclogged.

CHAPTER THREE

It was pushing his luck to travel openly. There could be Sov patrols. Sturgis knew that the Reds were trying to clear all major roads for their own vehicles. And there were more marauders out there looking to prey on any travelers, to steal their supplies—there were even cannibals. He had seen some survivors that had sunk that low, only last month. He'd killed them.

But he was overdue getting back to Okefenokee Base. And any other way would be too slow. He didn't have food for a long trek.

Three quarters of the way back to the Okefenokee, 112 miles later, at about Tifton, Georgia, Sturgis hung a left onto the tar of old Route 7, the road that intersected the Civil War-Era plantation canal he was looking for. It led to the part of the swamp in which Refuge Island, the C.A.D.S. base, lay hidden. His detailed map had been burned up in his suit fire. He hoped he remembered enough of the way to the canal and beyond—through the zigzagging streams of the swamp. His plan was to build a raft or find a boat. Maybe, just maybe, he could find Refuge Island.

The car engine started to sputter. He glanced at the gas gauge. The needle was below empty. The motor died and the car coasted to a stop. The canal was somewhere miles ahead. He had no idea how far. It could be fifteen miles or fifty. It was too dangerous to just walk the road.

He decided, after a moment's consideration to find the canal by cutting cross-country.

The Tech Commando emerged from his ancient VW, and after checking his .45—only five bullets left—consulted his compass. He took a blanket from the back seat and cut a slit in the middle of it, put it on as a poncho. It was getting to be a chilly day and it would be damper in the swamp. He started walking south—dead south, hoping to cut diagonally through the scrub pine woods without getting himself lost. On Route 7, he was an easy target.

He'd have to walk as far as he could before nightfall. The land around here was filled with brackish pools and fallen trees. Not to mention the plethora of snakes and alligators.

Over the next hours he slogged in everything from six inches of water to a foot of mud, always checking the compass. Sometimes the terrain was dry and grassy, the going easy. He circled the pools of putrescent green stagnation. It would have been tough going anyway, but the wound on his side ached and burned as he walked, adding to his discomfort. Sturgis had almost forgotten it while riding in the bucket seat of the VW. It began throbbing again.

He paused on a grassy area to check his compass again—and his watch. He'd been on a steady, straight bearing for over six hours. Surely he should have intersected the canal by now!

He continued walking. Up ahead of him were some dead saplings. The two-inch-wide stems might be dry enough for a campfire, and he could build a small night shelter. The last rays of the fading sun were disappearing in the shadows of the forest. Even on the pines, moss hung in long clumps from the branches. Using the moss to cover the dry sticks, Sturgis quickly made a wigwam type of shelter. It would do, he thought, unless it rained. He wrapped himself up in the "poncho" from the car and after warming his wet feet by the small fire he lit, he bedded down, .45 next to his hand.

He awoke stiff and hungry to the din of swamp birds calling. The raucous sounds grated his nerves. He checked his wound—still sore but no sign of infection. Then he reached into his pocket and pulled out the crumpled cigarette pack he had found in the car along with the matches. He lit it. *Horrible.* He spat it out, crumpled up the pack, and tossed it. He took a compass bearing and headed south—again. Maybe he had misjudged the distance . . . The woods he walked through for the first three hours were dry and pleasant smelling—a pleasure after yesterday. But in time it became marshy. Again he found himself sloshing through muddy water. He was hungry. Thirsty. Where was the canal? Maybe he just *thought* he was heading south. Maybe the compass was broken. He could be walking in circles.

He cleared away such thoughts. The compass had been okay yesterday, up north. It was just his fatigue depressing his mood. He had to stay alert. But his legs felt like lead weights. Sometimes it was all he could do to put one leg in front of the other. Still, he kept moving. After another half-hour, Sturgis saw a grassy clearing. A break in the slogging. It would be good to walk on some dry land for a while. It had to be better than slogging through the muck. He strode right out onto the grass and realized too late he'd made a mistake. A fatal mistake. The "grass" gave way under him. He was sinking. And he didn't stop sinking. *Quicksand!*

Think! Who had time to think? He was already up to his waist. He had to find something to grab onto. He knew if he struggled it would only make things worse. There was nothing he could see to grab. He kept sinking. He could actually feel the sand sucking him down. He had to do something. Sturgis shouted, "Over here. I'm in quicksand. Help." He felt almost foolish, for surely the swamp was deserted. *Do something else.* What? He'd read that in *some* quicksand you could swim. It was worth a try. He was now chest deep. He tried to lay his body forward, as if to swim. That brought muck up to his face, but it didn't seem to slow down the sinking. Every movement seemed to increase the pull on him. There were only seconds left, he knew that.

Then he thought he heard a whirring sound. An airboat? It could be an enemy. They might shoot him, but a "might" was better than the definite predicament he was in. "Hey, over here!"

The whirring sound grew louder. Finally he could detect a stirring in the tall reeds at the opposite bank. It was now or never. "Over here!" he yelled. The strange whirring stopped. "Help," Sturgis yelled. "I'm sinking in quicksand!"

There was that whirring sound again. Sturgis could see the tall swamp cattails waving as the dark squat figure moved closer. "Hurry!" Sturgis yelled.

After what seemed like an eternity, the cattails parted and pushed down to reveal a white-bearded man wearing a wide-brim straw hat, sitting in a wheelchair—an *electric* wheelchair. That's what Sturgis had heard. The man was alone. How could a man in a wheelchair help?

"Hold your horses, sonny . . . I got some rope. You just don't sink now, ya hear, boy? You just don't move now. Get ready to catch my rope." The voice had a deep timbre, was calm and authoritative.

"Right!" Sturgis yelled.

The old man pushed off the black wool blanket over his lap, grunted. His breath frosted in the chill morning air. He was fishing behind him on the chair. Finally he smiled. "Got everything on this here wheelchair, sonny . . . including a TV set . . . but I guess you're more interested in the rope."

Sturgis's mouth was filling with muck. His eyes were still above the surface. He watched as the man secured one end of the rope to a strong sapling immediately next to the wheelchair. "Okay . . . get ready to ketch, young fella." The man in the chair made a pretty good toss. Still, the distance was a good twenty feet and the rope fell short. The old man frowned, spat out his cigar, and said, "This takes a bit of concentrating." He quickly retrieved the rope, coiling it for another throw.

The rope sailed out again and this time Sturgis caught it, lifting up his sopping-wet arms, seizing it with his left hand.

Adding the strength of his right arm, he pulled himself across the distance. His legs sucked out of the muck, and lying flat now, he skidded over the slimy surface until his right hand clutched the sapling. Dropping the rope, he pulled himself up onto dry land, gasping and spitting out mud.

"Thanks," Sturgis said as he got up into a crouch. He was dizzy from the exertion.

"Don't mention it." The man tipped his hat with his left hand, "Glad to be of service."

Sturgis saw the face of a man in his sixties, a gray crew cut over a knitted brow.

Sturgis made to stand up. The old man pulled a revolver.

"Now, just you hold on there. That's a gun holstered to your belt. Who the hell are you? A Red?"

"No. An American: Colonel Dean Sturgis, U.S.A.F."

"*Ha*. Throw the gun away. Move real slow with your left hand."

"Just a second," Sturgis replied. "How do I know who *you* are? Even if you're an American—you sound like one—lots have turned collaborator."

"You *don't* know. But I ain't. Now, you don't have any options, son. Throw the gun far away—with your left hand, backwards-like."

Sturgis did as he was ordered, threw the gun about twenty feet into the woods. Wet as it was, it probably wouldn't fire anyway.

Deep black-pupiled eyes flashed with excitement. The old man squinted. "Now let's go through this, real slow. Who'd you say you were, sonny?"

"Dean Sturgis, Colonel, U.S.A.F."

The man cocked the revolver. "Not enough, son. *More.*"

"Until I know who the hell you are, I will only give my name, rank, and serial number. Even if I knew who you were . . . My outfit, mission—everything is secret."

"Secret? That's not the right attitude to take with me, sonny. I can help you, *if* you are who you say." He drew the wheelchair up closer. "Where you from, boy? Or is that a secret too?"

"I've got something in my coveralls that might help identify me."

"Okay, but stand up real slow. And just in case you think you can rush me figgering this little gun might miss . . ." The man pulled up the dangling black wool blanket. Two gleaming gun barrels were displayed, one on each side of the pants legs.

"These here are .30 caliber machine guns, sonny, and the triggers are in the armrest. Comprendez?"

"I read you loud and clear," Sturgis frowned. He reached slowly into his sodden coveralls and pulled out the ziplock bag. It was covered with gunk and was wet, but the contents were dry. He handed the old man the note from Robin and her picture.

The wheelchairman took them both carefully, whirred back five feet.

"Mighty fine gal, son. And a nice note—but how do I know she's really writing this letter to *you*? You still ain't proved you're a U.S. officer. Ya got any *military* I.D.?"

"I'd appreciate it if you'd hand that note back. With the picture, it's all I have of Robin. It's very important to me. I'm in a special unit, and that's all you need to know," Sturgis said, growing hot under the collar. "Who are you?" he demanded. "Are you a Revenger? Where's *your* I.D.?"

At the mention of the Revengers—the name for the U.S. Freedom Fighters in the southeast U.S.—the old man's eyes flickered. "I got this gun, boy. That's all the I.D. I need around here. Now, this conversation's been going in damned circles. You mentioned something about the Revengers. Do you know any?" he asked warily, "–by name? How about it, Colonel Sturgis?"

At last we're on to something, thought Sturgis. "Yes! There's Bart McCoy, a man in his early twenties with a patch over one eye. Jake McCoy is his brother and the actual leader. . . . There's a big guy, six feet five inches tall, must weigh about three hundred pounds. Anson's his name. I enlisted their aid when we attacked Charleston a few months ago."

There was a flicker of recognition in the old man's eyes. "That big guy you spoke of. Do you remember anything else about him?"

Sturgis frowned. "Well, he wore sunglasses all the time because he was self-conscious about the scars around his eyes. Is that what you mean? Don't ask me where they are, or how many. I won't answer."

The old man nodded. "Go on," he said, "you can leave out addresses. You're starting to make me believe you."

"Good. There are the Hatfields, led by Duke Hatfield, who stopped feuding with the Revengers and joined up with them a while ago." Sturgis racked his brain. What else was there? "There was a special unit called the Jeff Davis Squadron, that died to a man. The McCoys . . . they have this big cave . . ."

"You've seen that? What's it look like? I've been there."

"Well, it's full of beautiful crystals . . ."

The old man uncocked the pistol. "*Hell*, you must be an American. Those Revengers wouldn't let a

Ruskie or traitor live to tell the story if he'd seen the *Crystal Cave.*" He leaned forward and stared hard into Sturgis's eyes. "Are you one of them there *Blacksuits* that I heard so much about?"

Sturgis nodded.

The old man covered the machine-gun nozzles and put the revolver back on his lap. "I'd be proud to shake hands with you, sonny. My name is Peppercorn. Boss Peppercorn. I'm inviting you to my house, son. Got some moonshine licker and some interestin' doodads to show ya—just about a half-mile away."

Sturgis smiled. "I'd like that, but first let me retrieve my forty-five. And hand me back my letter and Robin's picture."

Peppercorn laughed. "Anything you say, sonny." After Sturgis got the gun, he handed Sturgis Robin's letter and picture. "Any friend of the Revengers is a friend of mine. Now, let's go—follow me."

With that he wheeled about. The whirring electric-battery-driven motor propelled the wheels at a good clip down a path, which Sturgis hadn't noticed before, for it was overhung by the tall reeds. "This way, ya heah? Come on, and get the lead out," Peppercorn yelled over his shoulder. Sturgis followed obediently.

The wheelchair sped down the path. Sturgis was still spitting mud and wishing the hell he could get the sloshy boots off. He had a hard time keeping up. He had no choice but to trust the old codger. And for some reason he did, anyway.

After ten minutes he saw the house silhouetted

against the sky on a rise: a big white-shingled ramshackle frame house set in a small clearing. Ramshackle mansion, that's what it should be called, he thought.

Peppercorn wheeled himself up a creaky board ramp laid atop stairs. It led up to the shaky clapboard porch filled with potted plants—dracaenas and philodendrons. Sturgis remembered seeing those plants in every damned government and contractor's office he'd ever been in pleading for better equipment for his men—before it had become too late.

Peppercorn rolled past the rusty porch swing and opened the screen door. Sturgis tried to help Peppercorn open the inner wooden door, but Peppercorn pushed Sturgis's hand away and bumped over the threshold on his own. As Sturgis was about to follow, Peppercorn said sternly, "You wait here. I'm not going to let you track up my house with your muddy boots. You just kick them off and strip that there mucky outfit off. I'll get you some duds."

Sturgis did as he was told, thankful to get his wet clothes off, but it was freezing on the porch. A few minutes later Sturgis heard the whirring sound of the wheelchair. Peppercorn opened the screen door and threw Sturgis some wide work pants and a blue plaid shirt. "Put these on. Ya don't mind walking barefoot, do you? Keep a lookout for swamp snakes, though. They's everywhere, even get in the house." Sturgis dressed quickly and stepped warily into the house. The screen door slammed behind him.

The place needed dusting, and the thin, worn old carpet must have hid a plentitude of loose boards, from the sound of it. But it was a sprawling open sunny sort of old house and was quite pleasant.

"Have a seat on that sofa and I'll join you . . . Gotta get some refreshments from the 'fridge. Got a generator in the cellar—that's the humming sound you hear," Peppercorn added by way of explanation. His voice trailed off to the kitchen, and he disappeared through the doorway.

Sturgis sank into the plush overstuffed paisley affair. It was so good to rest his weary bones. He put his bare feet up on an ottoman covered with snakeskin. Ecstasy! He looked around him as he heard clinking and slamming of cabinets and muttered curse words coming from the direction of the kitchen. The place was full of swamp stuff. There were some very large alligator pelts strung all over the peeling walls. The lamps on the end tables were made of coiled water moccasins. Horns, skins, and furs of practically everything that walked, crawled, or flew over the swamp were either mounted on the walls or cluttering the room like Victorian knickknacks.

Peppercorn returned with a tray bearing a cut-glass decanter and some snifters. And—best of all—some sandwiches. Looked like baloney. Sturgis didn't care. It was food!

"Glass set was my wife's. Hadn't had an occasion special enough to use this in a month or so . . . My wife used to use it for what she liked to call 'Special

Company.' " He put the tray down on the coffee table and turned up the kerosene hurricane lamp. "You don't like to sit in the dim, do you, son?" Sturgis wagged his head no. Peppercorn decanted a white clear liquid into the glasses. "Here's to better times, Colonel Dean Sturgis."

They downed their glasses. It was like liquid fire to Sturgis, but he needed it badly after dealing with the bikers and the long trek, not to mention the quicksand—and Peppercorn, himself.

"How's that taste? Puts hair on your lungs, boy. It does!"

"Sure does. I'll have another," said Sturgis.

Peppercorn smiled. "I knew you were my kind of man. Here." He filled their glasses again. "Made it myself. It's a special formula handed down from generation to generation." He took a swig and then took out a cigar and lit it. A look of contentment passed over his face. "Want one?"

Sturgis said, "Why not?" He let Peppercorn light it. It was too strong to inhale, but he puffed away. All the comforts of home. He lifted up a sandwich and demolished it, took another. It *was* baloney.

"How long have you been living here?" asked Sturgis.

"All my life, boy, all my life. Never had no cause to leave. The swamp's been good to me—'cept the time the alligator snapped my spine, I suppose. Swamp gave me what I needed to raise three boys and a girl. They got's all fancy and moved north. Said it was slow around here. Yup, this swamp is my home. Everything now come out like it was summer. Nukes hardly bothered the Okefenokee! My groves blossomed, fruits I never saw before popped out everywhere—snakes and monkeys by the carload. Had a hell of a time keeping the frogs from getting in the house . . . never saw so many."

Sturgis frowned. "The radioactivity is playing tricks. Up north everything is dead. I don't know if anything will come out up there this spring or this summer. Our scientists seem to think there might never be a real spring or summer, just a cold winter and a warmer winter. This swamp is some odd exception."

A look of concern crossed the ruddy face.

"For how long do they say the weird weather will last?"

"They don't know—could be forever."

Peppercorn frowned. "I heard it could be bad. . . . With the cold and the radioactivity, what are people going to eat? They can't grow nothin' in that."

"It's a big problem. You're lucky here, because of the swamp gases, I suspect. They keep the place warm. Out west, beyond the Mississippi, there might be a chance. But the East is hard hit. Millions of people are still dying from radiation burns and millions more are starving to death."

The old man's face grew ashen. Then he said in a quiet voice, "Can the human race survive, Colonel Sturgis? And *can we defeat the Reds*?"

"Would have been better if the nukes had never dropped. But they *did.* Most we can do now is try to pick up the pieces," Sturgis replied. "No real victory is possible anymore. *Real* victory would have been never having World War Three."

"But it was inevitable, wasn't it?" asked the old man, "—Owing to human nature." He puffed on the cigar, looking pleased, feeling he had made a good point.

Sturgis paused for a long time, then said, "I'm not so sure. I've seen a lot of *good* human nature as well as the worst . . . Since I've been fighting the invaders, I've met a lot of good people; Americans who were unselfish, strong, compassionate."

"What would you have done to stop the war, Colonel?"

"Well—as a Monday-morning quarterback? I would have locked the U.S. President and the Soviet Premier in a room without a view for as long as it took for them to come up with a fair agreement for disarmament and peace. Maybe put, say, the Dali Lama or someone in there with them as a mediator. Someone neutral, determined. They couldn't come out until they achieved peace. They couldn't have anything but bread and water until they had a fair, sound agreement."

"Interestin' idea, Colonel," Peppercorn chuckled. "I believe it *might* have worked," he said, slapping his leg for emphasis. "By god, I'd 've voted for that. Indeed I would've, Colonel Sturgis!"

"Yeah," Sturgis said, downing the last of his white lightning and putting his glass down. "Too bad no one thought of it last year!"

The old man harrumphed. "I suppose you have some questions. Shoot."

"Are there any Reds around here?"

"Hell, no!" He puffed his cigar and spat on the floor. "Let me explain myself a little to you, Colonel Sturgis. The Revengers done found me here. Said they'd like to use my house from time to time when they were on missions to the south. I begged to join them, but they said I wasn't mobile enough. So"—he paused to take another puff—"I'm just monitoring the broadcasts here with this here TV and CB Radio and stuff you see over there along the wall. It's all attached to tape recorders. Mostly all I hear is Red propaganda. I get bored with it, so's I machined me some special weaponry and electric motors. With stuff the Revengers brought to me, I was able to make this special shooting, speeding *wheelchair man-o'-war*. Just when I proved to the Revengers I could go with them on a mission, I come down with a tetch of swamp fever. . . . So, I'm still here. But I'm well now. My white lightnin' and snake oil *got* me well. But the Revengers won't be back till a month's gone by. I'm just itchin' to get into action."

"I'm kinda glad you stuck around. Thanks to you—"

"Don't mention it, boy. Besides, I like your company. Where are my manners? Want some more sandwiches? Were six enough? I got some crackers in the jar on the table in the kitchen and some dried jerky too. And a coupla cans of—"

"This will do," Sturgis said, taking another sandwich, chasing it with a slug of moonshine.

Suddenly there was a click and the large color TV set turned on.

"Got it on automatic timer," explained Peppercorn. "Time to translate Jerry Jeff Jeeters—you know about him?"

Sturgis nodded.

Peppercorn watched the show intently. He began scribbling down the Bible verses Reverend Jeeters quoted. Jeeters was a flamboyant country-preacher-type minister. The Reds thought that Jerry Jeff Jeeters was a turncoat. All of the reverend's near-hysterical bible-pounding preachings extolled the Soviet nuke strike. But the Reds didn't know what the Revengers, and what the C.A.D.S. commander knew: Jeeters was in fact passing on information to the U.S. freedom fighters in a biblical code. That code was quite easy to decipher, once you caught on how.

Not for the first time Sturgis watched the silver-haired Reverend Jeeters, in his red glitter-sharkskin suit and blue neon tie with a tie tack depicting Christ on the cross. He was on his knees now, with his hands upraised in a supplicating gesture. "Verily I say unto you, the Lord has given our Russian brothers to heal us. They have taken our sins upon their shoulders."

He bowed his head as if in silent prayer, stood up slowly and walked to his pink leatherette chair. Jeeters placed pince-nez reading glasses over his wide eyes, collapsed into his leatherette recliner. He began reading chapter and verse of the Bible to prove his point. "Take James, verse twelve . . . "

After a half-hour Peppercorn had a whole list of numbers on his pad. He turned off the 27-inch TV after Jeeters finished his reading (by tearing off his shirt and throwing it down on the floor and collapsing in religious ecstasy).

"Good showman, huh?" Peppercorn laughed. "We'll translate that now." He looked up the verses in his Bible and decoded: It showed the Cubans were on the move, occupying something, somewhere. Peppercorn picked up his pad and read slowly, " 'Animals-Dreams-in-Land-of-Forever-Youth?' What do you make of that, Colonel?"

"I think he means Disney World," Sturgis replied. "Florida's the land of the Fountain of Youth."

"I agree," Peppercorn said. "Where were we? Oh, yes—What have you been up to? Can you use that information? Where is your unit?"

"Seems like I should trust you, Peppercorn. I'll have you know we share the same swamp. Do you know of an island in the Okefenokee that has some ruins on it? That's the place I'm looking for. That's our base—Refuge Island, we call it."

"Hell." Peppercorn shook his head. "There's half a hundred places in this here swamp that fits that description."

Sturgis slumped. "I was hoping you could get me there."

How could Sturgis find it without the superb guidance instruments of his C.A.D.S. suits? Peppercorn said suddenly, "I've had too much of the white lightnin'—I hear the strangest sound! Do you hear that?"

"Yes!" A look of hope came to Sturgis's face. *Could it be?*

"I've been hearing that sound every night for a coupla weeks. It's kind of a strange nasal, whirring sound. Now what sort of animal would make that noise?"

Sturgis listened some more and then he joyfully recognized it. "Peppercorn, do you have a boat?"

"I sure have. Why?"

"I think I can find Refuge Island."

"I'm fit and itchin' to travel. These here hands are as strong as steel. I'm capable of *anything*. Let's go, Sturgis."

CHAPTER FOUR

"I can *show* you what that weird sound is, Peppercorn. If we hurry. We mustn't let one second delay us." Sturgis slipped on his mucky boots and grabbed his pistol off the porch swing.

The Commando and the old swampman cut down the sloping, overgrown lawn to the little dock on the water. "You'll have to give me a hand getting the consarned chair into the boat," Peppercorn apologized. "There's a couple of boards in the boat I use as a ramp—when someone can help me. Tried it alone one time—nearly drowned. But I don't go anywhere without my fighting wheelchair."

Sturgis did as suggested, making sure the makeshift ramp was sturdily stretched to the small dock. The twelve footer with one outboard Johnson sure needed a coat of paint, but it looked fit enough—if he could get the old man in without tipping it.

In a matter of a minute or two he managed. Then he got in himself, in the stern. The small boat steadied. It was low in the water, but it was even.

"Don't forget the boards, Sturgis. Got to get me out at the other end—Where are we going?"

"To the source of that noise. You just sit tight." Sturgis pulled on the rope and the Johnson roared to life. He took the rudder and steered them out into the algae-green channel. He wound through several turns, trying to follow the sound. He thought it was close-by—maybe a mile or less. The colonel wished the hell he had the sophisticated direction-finding sensors of the C.A.D.S. suit. But he didn't. Suddenly the sound ceased.

"Fenton, you bastard," Sturgis cursed, "Keep playing your bagpipe!"

"Is that what the hell that sound is?" exclaimed Peppercorn. "I thought it was a camel in heat!"

Sturgis cut power and waited, dead-still in the water. "Maybe he's filling the bag with air," he muttered. "The damned Brit shouldn't be playing the thing—it's a breach of security. But I'm glad he is. I know we're close to base now."

"Don't be too sure, son. Sounds carry for miles and miles in these parts."

The mournful wail started up again. The colonel decided it was up to the right, past a reedy area ahead, and turned that way.

"Sturgis," Peppercorn suggested, "might I inform you that we are about to hit a mudbank? Could you slow down a bit? Take the long way around—to the left."

Sturgis, though impatient, did as the old swampman suggested. The bagpipes kept sounding. Sturgis, after another half-hour of churning the silted waters of the Okefenokee, realized he was no closer than before. The swamp was a maze. The compass Sturgis held in the palm of his hand spun due to the magnetic interference of the swamp gases. The swamp gas produced a lot of odd phenomena. There was little chance of finding Refuge Island when he didn't even know in what direction they were heading; and the swamp was full of echoes that distorted the direction and distance of the pipes. Suddenly Sturgis remembered Billy had led them into the swamp along an *old barge canal.* Their water-churning tribikes had found one particular stream from the end of the canal into a lake. . . .

"Peppercorn, do you know of an old canal that leads into these waters from the north? If we can find the end of that canal then I think we can get somewhere from there."

"There were hundreds serving the old plantations around Civil War times. Most have totally disappeared."

"It's a really old thing that is always overflowing its banks," Sturgis said. "It's about fifty feet wide. Think, Peppercorn. We found it by turning west on Route Seven, near Makachopee. At a highway culvert bridge—at the junction of a small dirt road. It leads to some streams after fifty miles or so—and any one of those streams leads into this wide muck-filled stagnant lake—lily pads, bordered by big cypress trees covered with vines—there was another bunch of streams heading south on the other side of the lake, heading south. *Think.* You must know it."

Peppercorn said, "Why, that must be Corcorans' Canal. Damned, it must be. Is it chock-full of alligators and snakes?"

"Sounds like it," Sturgis replied. "Do you know the way to the lake at the end of Corcorans' Canal from here? Before I get us totally lost?"

"Darn right I do, son—you just let me direct you from now on. You damned near got me lost with all your guessing." The bagpipes ceased once more. The colonel hoped Peppercorn knew what he was doing, for it was getting dark.

Two hours later Sturgis watched irregular dark clouds roll over the half-moon above. Huge cypress tree limbs overhung the very narrow passage. Peppercorn told Sturgis where to steer, though it was utterly black. Finally it got so dark even the old swampman couldn't see a thing. He pulled a flashlight out of his wheelchair's storage space, and he played it over the misty area ahead. Sturgis was sure they were hopelessly lost.

The frogs grew so loud that they could hardly hear their noisy motor. Fruit bats flitted in the flashlight beam.

"Are you sure you know where we are?" Sturgis asked. "Seems to me we've been going in circles and—"

A six-foot-long black snake dropped from a tree branch onto Peppercorn's blanketed lap. He grabbed it with lightning speed just below its head. "Pretty boy, you gotta go back into the water," the old man said softly, and dropped it overboard. Sturgis stopped asking questions and just followed the old man's directions.

Sturgis was amazed at the old man's calmness and his certitude. In about forty more minutes they heard splashes. The light revealed two big alligators sliding off a muddy bank and heading for the boat.

"Steer a bit into the center of the channel, these boys ain't hungry or they'd move faster," Peppercorn advised softly.

With these words Peppercorn pulled a walking stick out from under his black blanket and whopped the first 'gator on the nose. The 'gators turned around and sailed away, as if embarrassed.

The little boat continued onward. It seemed that nothing fazed Boss Peppercorn, thought Sturgis, perhaps that's why he's called *Boss*.

They managed to navigate through a bewildering set of twists and turns for another hour and came out into the calm moonlit lake. Sturgis recognized the beautiful place almost immediately. There were even torn patches of lily pads from the passage of all the tribikes and the Rhino.* "This is *it*—the oblong lake bordered by the tall pines. And there's the end of the canal!" he pointed. "Over there, Billy took us down the second stream out of the lake. The stream that heads east by southeast."

They were no longer lost. Sturgis felt relaxed for the first time since they set off on the water journey.

In a short time he sighted the steep-banked Refuge Island.

"Home sweet home!"

*Rhino—an all-terrain battlewagon (see *C.A.D.S. No. 2*)

CHAPTER FIVE

Sturgis steered the little boat along the steep root-snared banks of Refuge Island. There must be guards posted, he thought. Could something be wrong? In the first light of dawn he found the sandy rutted area where the tribikes came up out of the water. This was the place, all right. He got close to the little red sand beach and cut the motor. He waded in and tied the bow of the boat to a jutting root at the edge of the little beach. "Back in a minute, Peppercorn."

"Now you just wait a damned minute, Sturgis. I want out of this boat. If there's any trouble I couldn't help save your ass again unless I'm on dry land—take the damned boards out of the bottom of the boat and make a ramp for me. Get me the hell up on the beach."

Suddenly there was a rustling in the vines and brambles to their left. A black-suited figure emerged. He had an AMERICA—LOVE IT OR LEAVE IT bumper sticker, much the worse for wear, plastered across the breastplate.

"Tranh! It's me, Sturgis, and a friend."

Peppercorn put down the blanket. He had uncovered his twin submarine guns just in case. "Hell, then," Peppercorn yelled, "If you're a *friend*, then help the colonel get me the hell onto shore."

Tranh snapped up his visor, smiled. "It's great to see you, Commander! We'd almost given you up for lost."

"I had some troubles. Lost my suit, but I managed to blow it up. The tribike too."

"Save your chatter, boys, and get me on dry land."

Tranh laughed and said, "Hold your horses, old-timer, and I'll lift you and your wheelchair right up and onto shore."

"I don't think you could be that strong, my boy."

Tranh laughed. "The musculature-assist servo-mechanisms do the work, old-timer." And with those words, he waded alongside the boat and lifted Peppercorn and his chair up to neck level, steady and level as could be, and walked ashore with him and put him down. Peppercorn was amazed. "Say, you guys got quite an invention there. How much a suit like that cost?"

"Neighborhood of twelve million dollars," said Tranh. "Well worth it."

Peppercorn grew silent for a moment and had a faraway look. Then he smiled. "Say, listen, boy—maybe you got a *used* one you can sell cheap to an old paraplegic . . . so's he can walk around again—right?"

Sturgis said, "It's a thought. We'll talk about it if we ever get a spare. Right now, let's get back to the encampment. Is there anything new, Tranh?"

"A hell of a lot," the Vietnamese-born man said with a slight Asiatic softness to his vowels. "We've established contact by a secret satellite channel with White Sands. They're making progress out there contacting a lot of small isolated U.S. bases still intact, all over the West. There's a lot more news too. Fenton—"

"Lead on, then, Tranh—I've forgotten which one of these mazes of paths through the tall grass leads to the clearing. I'll want a full briefing."

On the way back to the C.A.D.S. temporary headquarters at the center of the island, Sturgis filled his right-hand man in on what had happened to him and just who Boss Peppercorn was. Peppercorn cussed and swore, for everytime the narrow dirt path twisted sharply, his wheels got stuck in the leaning-over tall grass. "Gotta trim back these weeds, boy, ain't a fit path."

Tranh agreed. "We're short of gardeners. Maybe we can put you to work on it—can you swing a scythe in that chair?"

That shut up Peppercorn's complaining!

Tranh snapped his helmet shut and announced over his boom-mike, "STURGIS IS BACK." People came running out of a series of low rock-and-thatch huts shouting their greetings. One of the first to reach them was Fenton, his coveralls all covered with grease. The big Brit still had a monkey wrench in his hands. "Dean, for god's sake, you're still alive." He threw his arms around the colonel, patting him on the back. "Welcome back—we thought—"

"I know," said the colonel. "It was damned near the truth."

He introduced Peppercorn to Fenton and also to Billy, Roberto, Rossiter, and the others that came out to greet them. Then Sturgis said, "Why isn't there a lookout? Don't you think we need one, Tranh? I made a heck of a noise coming up on the island, and not a Blacksuit to be seen until you came along. If I was the enemy . . ."

Tranh said, "It's my fault. I'm in charge. It's just that there was a lot of excitement an hour ago when we raised White Sands on the Rhino's radio set. I was the lookout over at the beach, but when I heard on the helmet radio that White Sands—"

"We all make mistakes, Tranh," Sturgis said sternly. "Including Fenton here. You must stop playing the pipes. You can hear it for miles! Both of you have a mild reprimand noted on your records." He smiled. "Now, what about this commlink with White Sands? Fenton—fill me in—over in my hut."

Sturgis arranged for Peppercorn to be shown around and then he and Fenton went into a long partially-dug-in command building—little more than a stone wall with a thatch roof—and talked over steaming cups of coffee.

"It's an incredible stroke of luck, Dean," the excited Britisher said, leaning over the rough-hewn table. "There was a Telos communications satellite launched just before the nuke attack. Though all our other satellites were knocked out of commission by the Reds, this one wasn't in orbit yet, so it isn't damaged. President Williamson has had someone trying to get it operational from the minute he knew it was up there. Now White Sands has a scrambled, ultra-high-frequency way to contact us directly—and to contact any U.S. force with the new Z-decoder diodes in its radio set. The Rhino's had the capability all this time, and so has White Sands—but we didn't know it was there, and we didn't know the frequency. We have the President's science adviser, Gridley, to thank for figuring out the whole thing. The satellite was tumbling also. Gridley figured out a way to stabilize it by radio command so it could be made operational."

"What's the news from White Sands?"

"You can talk to them direct. Come to the Rhino—it's crisp and clear, despite the swamp-gas interference, due to its high frequency."

Inside the confines of the spherical-wheeled Rhino, Sturgis put on the headphones and Fenton punched in the numbers on the console. "Just like making a long-distance call." He smiled. "Except the Reds don't know the area code!"

"White Sands Base," came a dry voice. "Reading you."

"This is Colonel Sturgis. Give me the highest officer on duty, or the President."

"*Yessir.*"

In a few seconds the President himself picked up. The wiley Oklahoman who Sturgis had come to respect and have confidence in said, "I'm glad you're alive, Colonel. We heard . . . you were . . . lost."

"Thank you, sir, I'm found now. I just got back. Are you absolutely sure the Reds can't hear us?"

"Gridley informs me they don't even know this channel exists. Besides, there is a way to detect if we're being picked up. . . ."

"Great. My congratulations to old Gridley and your entire staff. Now, what are your orders, sir?"

The voice grew grimmer. "Colonel. You've been through a lot, from what Fenton reported to me a few hours ago. It is beyond any expression of gratitude that I can express. But now our intelligence reports that there is a Cuban presence—in force—near Orlando. They're using the Epcot Center of the Disney World complex as a ready-made base. This is according to decoded messages from Reverend Jeeters. You know how reliable his information has been in the past."

"Yes, he's a brave man—real patriot."

"Well, if we could resupply you by air, Colonel, supply you with every type of ammo . . . possibly some laser rifles too—the LWAs you have such high praise for—could you go down there and blow the hell out of them? Before they settle in and make the base impregnable? This isn't an order, Colonel. It's a . . . hope. A request. For you've done so much already."

Sturgis looked at Fenton. Fenton winked.

Sturgis smiled. "Sure, Mr. President. If we get an airdrop of supplies and especially some LWAs. . . . Have you heard how many casualties we've had?"

"Yes. Over fifty percent. We can't replace them at this time. We're training new C.A.D.S. soldiers and manufacturing more suits. But we have the airlift capability *now*. We've been busy as beavers here refitting some old prop planes with low-level radar and night-flying capability. We've acquired the fuel, built wingtip tanks to extend their range. We can have an airdrop to you within twelve hours."

Sturgis said, "If they are spotted . . . "

"The three special planes have no guns. They're slow and cumbersome to maneuver. If they're spotted by the Reds, they're incapable of defending themselves. But they *won't* be spotted. These old sky-boxcars can fly at treetop level, in the pitch-dark. They'll get to you. Just prepare a drop zone."

"Tell them they'll be welcome, Mr. President. I'll draw up a list of what we need, and Fenton will radio you in an hour with our shopping list. I'm sure every man in my unit will volunteer, as I will, for the mission to Epcot Center. Thank you, sir."

"Thank *you*, Colonel Sturgis. Over and out."

CHAPTER SIX

It sounded like a bombing raid. Suddenly the early-morning quiet of the Okefenokee Swamp was broken by the drone of prop-plane engines, and the air began whistling with the sound of heavy objects plummeting to earth through the fog.

"Look out, Billy!" shouted Tranh. "Heads down!" The Geometric Identification-mode radar in Tranh's C.A.D.S. suit had locked onto a large object hurtling from two hundred feet above straight for the younger man, who was still climbing into his bulky gear. Sturgis had ordered everyone to suit up, for safety.

Billy looked up and jumped to the right in the same split-second motion. The quick-witted West Virginian was barely able to avoid being smashed by the half-ton package. Billy had been too close to the water for a wrong move. But he'd managed to jump in the right direction. "Jesus! Can't those turkeys up there follow coordinates any better than that? I could have been alligator food!" He tested the shoulder that took the brunt of his fall and then struggled to his feet. The

Vietnamese-American helped him.

"Be glad we're getting this," Tranh confided. "We can't make it without supplies and ammo." Tranh, unlike Billy Dixon, had been quick to don his suit once the order was given. But he didn't rub it in.

Crates rained down all around them, punctuated by occasional splashes as impact-resistant crates struck the murky swamp waters instead of land. They materialized out of the heavy fog like meteors, unseen until just before they struck. The roar of the plane engines seemed magnified in the fog, sounding like an entire squadron was hurtling by the C.A.D.S. base.

Billy was soon into his suit and, like the rest of his fellow team members nearby, activated his radar and G.I. mode onto the flying objects and the opaque sky above. The G.I. mode identified three prop planes. They were C-47 Model 495s, ancient crafts that had been pulled out of a dusty storage hangar at White Sands. They hadn't been flown in decades, but they were the only planes available that could carry enough for the drop mission to the C.A.D.S. unit. A crew working around the clock for days had patched them together with stray spare parts to make them airworthy. The packages heaved out of the cargo bays by the C-47 crews were most of what Sturgis had ordered: spare parts, equipment, and ammunition vital to the survival of the C.A.D.S. men and the success of their coming mission against the Cubans at Disney World.

The supplies actually had been targeted for drop about a hundred and fifty meters from the C.A.D.S. base. But thick, wet fog obscured the swamp, and faulty equipment aboard the lead plane had resulted in a very scattered bombardment. By the time Sturgis frantically radioed the commanding pilot of his error, nearly all of the supplies had been tossed out of the planes.

Lousy airdrop, Sturgis fumed to himself as the packages thumped to earth. He stifled his criticism, however, reminding himself he was lucky to get anything at all. If not for the drop mission, they'd be in poor shape to defend themselves, let alone engage in combat at Disney World. Besides, the men in the planes had risked their own lives to carry out the drop, flying in at night low to the ground to avoid being detected by Soviet radar.

Luckily, no one on the ground was hurt, and nothing in the base was damaged.

The radio at Sturgis's ear crackled to life. "That's all there is," said the commanding pilot. "Sorry about the mistake in coordinates."

"No reported injuries," Sturgis answered gruffly. "But some of the boxes are in the water." He was not pleased about the idea of fishing packages out of alligator-infested waters.

"Everything's been packed water-repellent and impact-resistant," the pilot assured him. "They should float for hours."

"Roger. Any LWAs?" Sturgis was still hoping that somehow Van Patten, back at White Sands, had been able to conjure up more of the tricky but spectacularly effective liquid wave amplifier weapons. With LWAs, his men would be able to vaporize anything that stood in their way. But the lone one Sturgis possessed was dead, and Van Patten had not been hopeful of correcting the model's overheating defects soon.

"Negative on the LWAs," came the pilot's reply. "Dart missiles, E-balls, 9mm standard rounds, LPF flamethrower backtanks, helmet strobes, batteries, medical supplies, rations—no LWAs."

"Dammit," Sturgis said softly.

"Sorry, Colonel, technical problems in LWA manufacture."

"Not your fault. Thanks, Corwin. We'll take over from here."

"Roger. Wish I could drop you some C.A.D.S.-suited Commandos, too. Maybe next time. Any messages for the home base, sir?"

"I'll make contact directly later—over the Telos link."

"All right, sir. I'm going to get the hell out of here. Over and out." Above the fog, the drone of the prop engines rose in pitch as the planes moved west. The roar diminished and then ceased. The eeriness of the silence was heightened by the wet, foggy mists that wafted along the surface of the water and weaved among the moss-covered trees. The fog made it difficult, if not impossible, to see beyond a few yards.

"Okay, men," Sturgis said into his headset. "Let's not sit around like a bunch of old women waiting for tea. I want everything collected, examined, and inventoried right away. Tranh, you're in charge. There were twenty bundles scheduled to be dropped—make sure they're all accounted for." Sturgis headed for his base communications center, where he would raise President Williamson via Telos.

The wiry Vietnamese dispatched crews to search the tangled swamp brush for the precious packages. He saw right away that retrieving the ones from the water would be far more difficult. Tranh looked around. "Roberto," he called into his suit radio, "—come with me."

Roberto Fuentes sprang forward. He was agile and fast, one of the most expert of the C.A.D.S. men in manuevering in the heavy suits. Agility was just what Tranh needed.

Roberto and Tranh mounted their tribikes and eased them into the warm, slow-moving water. With its crust of algae, it looked like pea soup. The wide wheels of the bikes acted like ballast, keeping them afloat.

They circled the island twice, then Tranh's bike bumped something.

"Over here." Tranh pointed to a bulky package bobbing in the water. The two C.A.D.S. men maneuvered alongside the package. Even with the added advantage of the suits' power lifters in the arms, the crate was too bulky. Neither Tranh nor Fuentes could get into the right position for proper leverage without risk of tipping his bike. The crate kept slipping from their grasps like a greased pig at a country fair.

"Wait a minute," Tranh said. He pulled back to examine the situation. They could prod the box close to the shore, but someone would still have to wade into the water to haul it onto the land. The other team members might as well get in on the action.

"Those alligators will eat anything," objected

Fuentes. "I'm not sure I want to let this package float around."

Tranh blew out his breath noisily. "The only alternative is to devise some kind of grappling system. We could push the boxes toward shore and hold them there while someone on land latches onto them and hauls them up. We'd better hurry, too—no telling how long the water-repellent wrapping is going to last, or one of these 'gators decides to try one for lunch."

"Hey," Fuentes shouted, noticing his radar readout light up, "there's something coming at vector twelve—and closing fast!"

No sooner were the words out of his mouth than a boat shot out of the curtain of fog and made a neat circle around them, causing a ripple of waves to bounce the tribikes. Tranh and Roberto tensed. It was a fan boat, one of the type that belonged to the tribe of marauding swamp bandits who'd attacked the C.A.D.S. unit when it first stumbled upon the secluded swamp area.

But instead of bearing hostile savages, it was filled with four women. Dressed in animal pelts, belts hung with crude weapons, they looked like warriors. In the bow of the boat stood the leader, a woman of Amazonian proportions with her long and ragged dark hair flowing back from her face. She held a spear in front of her, and the look on her face said she was not to be taken lightly. Behind her, other fan boats buzzed into view in the now-clearing mists.

Van Noc and Fuentes breathed a collective sigh of relief. Both recognized the band as the once-captive women that Sturgis recently had freed from Macocco and his tribe of brutal, cannibalistic swamp dwellers. The women had been enslaved, abused, and sometimes eaten. Sturgis had whipped Macocco in hand-to-hand fighting, and now the women ruled the Okefenokee. And from the look of it, they had taken their new power to the hilt. They were tan and lean and well-armed.

The leader turned her fierce gaze on Tranh and Roberto, and for a fraction of a second, the C.A.D.S. men thought the visit might not be friendly after all.

"I am Dieter," the woman announced solemnly, breaking the tension. "We saw your objects fall from the sky. You need our help. We've located three of the sky-packages."

Van Noc and Fuentes looked at each other. Dieter and her band must be keeping an eye on the C.A.D.S. base, watching from hiding places in the vegetation-choked swamp. Now the grateful women were offering much-needed assistance.

Within hours, the "swamp cats," as Fuentes affectionately dubbed them, directed the C.A.D.S. men to all the packages that had fallen in the murky waters, and had helped them haul the boxes to shore. They were deft in handling their fan boats, zipping along the narrow channels and making quick, sure turns. They supplied primitive grapplers made of long poles securely mounted with hooks made of some of their ex-captors' carved bones.

All the while, alligators cruised the area, waiting for mistakes that meant meals. Their long forms darted back and forth just beneath the water's surface, and occasionally their bulbous eyes and flared nostrils poked out.

While Roberto and Tranh worked with the swamp women rounding up the supplies, Sturgis raised White Sands on the command center's radio, via the Telos satellite. He informed Science Adviser Gridley of the success of the airdrop.

"What's the status of the Liquid Wave Amplifer?" Sturgis asked. Perhaps there was still a chance the weapons could be airlifted to his unit at a later time.

"Bugs aren't worked out," said Gridley. "Just a moment—Van Patten's here. You can speak directly to him."

"Hello, Colonel," boomed the R&D chief's strong voice. "I wish I had better news for you. I've been working around the clock on the LWA, but I can't get rid of the overheating flaw. Any LWA I sent you would be a ticket to the cemetery."

"We need them anyway," Sturgis said. "The one I had is kaput. We'll take our chances. How many can you get out to us right away on another drop?"

There was nothing but static for a few moments. "I'm afraid it's not that simple," Van Patten said at last. "The prototype I gave you contained my last transphasor diodes. That one, at least, was rigged to give a warning when it overheated. I can't duplicate it, not yet. The ones here in the shop have been blowing up without any warning at all. It's too risky for any LWAs to be released."

"I'm the one who assesses the risks," Sturgis said.

"Colonel Sturgis," broke in Gridley, "the LWA is

still highly unreliable and not suitable for field use. I must add that we have lost two more men in tests."

Sturgis sighed. "How much longer do you think it will be before the defects are corrected? A guy could *use* a laser rifle around here. I should know."

"There's no telling," interjected Van Patten. "We're trying substitute diodes right now. Could solve the problem today—or maybe not for months."

"In *months,* Van Patten?" growled Sturgis. "In months, the Russians and Cubans will have more than a *toehold* in the U.S. unless I get those LWAs. You *know* they have to be beaten back *now,* before they increase their strength and numbers, and before radiation sickness claims the few able-bodied Americans who are left to fight. *Every* advantage counts!"

"We're all well aware of the situation we face," spoke up Gridley. Then he changed the subject. "When do you move against the Cuban base in Florida?—the President asked."

Sturgis snapped, "Too soon with too little firepower. Tell him we move out at twenty-one hundred tonight. Conditions permitting, I'll report in when we achieve our objective."

"God speed. The President said we can count on you."

"All right, let's go over the plan." By the light of a atomic power-pack lantern, Sturgis spread his Exxon roadmaps and sheets of scrawled notes on the ground before him. The maps were dog-eared and greasy with well-worn folds, but they were worth more than the gold in Fort Knox. They were possibly the only maps left in America of the area.

Hunched around Sturgis in the darkness were Peppercorn, Dixon, Fuentes, Van Noc, Rossiter, and MacLeish. "We leave in two hours," Sturgis said. He traced his finger down a black line on one of the maps. "We head southeast and pick up the highway to Jacksonville, and from there go almost due south, passing the lakes, until we arrive on the outskirts of Orlando. From Orlando, Disney World is about thirty miles south, but before we proceed, we'll send a scouting party."

"Will the highways be secure?" asked Rossiter.

"As secure as they are anywhere in this country." Sturgis thought of the gangs of Americans roaming the countryside, attacking other Americans. More often than he cared to remember, the C.A.D.S. team had had to fight off marauding American gangs as well as the Russian invaders.

"All indications are that we won't be bothered on the way. Our best info is that the Soviets haven't landed in Florida in any significant numbers, and the Commie Cubans don't have any troop concentrations there except for the base we're about to hit."

"Bloody Cubans have agreed to do the Russkies' dirty work for them. Mass murder in exchange for the rights to Florida, right Colonel?" said a livid Fenton MacLeish.

"Yeah, that seems to be the setup. And you can be damn well sure the Cubans are experts at bush and swamp guerilla fighting." Sturgis measured off a distance on the map with his thumb and forefinger.

"We've got about one hundred and fifty to two hundred miles to cover, and if we don't follow the highway, we'll have to pick our way through back roads and brush. We've got to get there fast if we're going to have any element of surprise. If all goes well, we'll make Orlando by dawn."

"Do you have any idea what the odds are?" asked Billy. "How many Cubans we'll be facing?"

"The Cubans are sure to outnumber us by as much as five or six to one. There's fifty-two of us here. We might be facing three hundred or more of them. We don't know what they're armed with. Any more questions?"

"Yeah," said Roberto. "Who's gonna watch the store while we're gone? Peppercorn?"

"No. Peppercorn's coming. We've got Dieter and her women to watch the base. Boss Peppercorn here has shown me that even in his wheelchair he's a guy worth having around. And I don't want him back here chasing the women around in his electric wheelchair." Sturgis grinned broadly as Peppercorn started to sputter an objection. "Just kidding about the women, Pepp. But seriously, Dieter and the women can watch the base."

"Hell, if they're so hot, why don't we send *them* to Orlando instead?" drawled Billy in an exaggerated Southern accent. "It's about time we got some equal-opportunity fighters in this outfit."

The men, including Sturgis, laughed. Then the colonel sobered. "It may come to that sooner than you think," he said. "Every man, woman, and child in America who is healthy enough to pick up a stick and use it is going to be called to action at some point. We're going to have to take help where we can get it." Sturgis reached into his chest pocket and pulled out a nearly flat cigarette pack. He took out the last cigarette, crumpled the pack, and held up the cigarette in the light of the lantern.

"Gentlemen, you are about to see the last of my nonradioactive cigs go up in smoke. I would never have come back to base so fast if I had realized there were no cigs."

It was just the moment Tranh had been waiting for. He pulled open a rucksack and spilled a dozen cartons of cigarettes into the lamplight. "They were in the drop," he crowed, pleased with his surprise. "They're clean, too—not even a fraction of a rad. They were found in the basement storage of a roadside grocery in the middle of Reno."

With cries of pleasure, everyone grabbed for the cigarettes. Sturgis pawed through the cartons. "These are low-tar cigs." He feigned outrage. "Not a Camel in the lot!" Even in the semidarkness, Tranh could see his commander's eyes twinkling happily.

The first part of the trek went slower than Sturgis had reckoned. It took a long time for the tribikes and Rhino to churn their way out of the swamp, following the moss- and mangrove-choked canals that sliced up the Okefenokee. Once they reached the highway to Jacksonville, they found they could not make use of the asphalt—the freeway was jammed with the vehicles of desperate Americans who had tried in vain to flee the nuclear disaster.

Swarms of gnats droned everywhere. The vehicles were in freeze-frame disarray on the road, like the carcasses of some herd-beasts that had swept in and died suddenly in one spot. Some cars and trucks had been abandoned. Others had become coffins. Rotting, huddled bodies visible through the windows took on a monsterlike appearance under the slim beams of the C.A.D.S. advance squad's lights. More bodies were sprawled along the road. A quick G.I. mode scan and telescopic probe showed that the grim train of cars and bodies went on for miles. The flies—millions of them—disturbed by the C.A.D.S. team, buzzed aloft.

"It must smell like hell here." Tranh muttered.

"And I can't get the Rhino through this mess," added Fenton. The Brit was driving the Rhino, and Peppercorn and Rossiter were inside the spherical-wheeled battlewagon with him.

Sturgis did a computer analysis of the surrounding terrain and studied the readout in his helmet. It didn't look too bad—mostly level ground with low brush. The G.I. mode would show up any obstacles well in front of them, red-flagging enemy personnel, if any.

"Fan out to the left of the road and follow the highway from the side. Whitman, take the lead. MacLeish, bring the Rhino up to the middle. Carter and Smith to the sides, Fuentes the rear. Keep all engines on mute and use infrared screens when necessary for tracking."

Slowly the C.A.D.S. formation moved out again in the night.

With the strobers and infrared tracking, which enabled them to spot all objects and gauge their size and distance, it was not difficult to move away from the impromptu cemetery on the roadway. If there had been any onlookers in the night, the high-tech warriors and their odd machines churning along the earth would have seemed like a strange robot army from another planet.

The silence of the night settled in around them as they rolled and bumped their way through the verdant Florida countryside. The green landscape had not yet suffered the withering, lethal effects of fallout. *Soon,* thought Sturgis. *Soon the radioactive rain will fall and this will all become another wasteland, too.*

His thoughts drifted on to Robin. He still ached that he'd come so close to finding her at Stone Mountain, only to miss her by days. At least she was safe—at the time she wrote the message. If Sturgis survived, God willing, he would try again. And again. He had to hold her in his arms soon.

Sturgis knew he couldn't stand to live in this nightmare world human stupidity had created much longer that unless he found her.

Suddenly the night was shattered by an explosion. Then another and another, lighting up the darkness at the front of the C.A.D.S. column with balls of flaming orange. Screams pierced everyone's ears. Still another explosion sent shock waves rocking the tribikes.

Silhouetted in the lightning of the blasts, Sturgis could see debris flung into the night air. The bits looked like pieces of C.A.D.S. suits and tribikes. His stomach churned.

"Halt!" he bellowed. "Defensive positions! Fire when necessary! Whitman! Whitman! Report in!" There was no answer—only moaning in the helmet radioes. As the soldiers quickly regrouped, Sturgis shot his tribike forward, weaving through the men.

Behind him, another explosion ripped the night, raining dirt and debris over a wide area. *What in the hell is going on?* Sturgis thought wildly. Were they under some kind of artillery attack? Why didn't their screens pick up the enemy?

He didn't have to wait for an answer. "Land mines!" someone ahead of him shrieked. "Land mines, Colonel! This is Rains. Whitman's been hit, sir!"

Sturgis slammed on his brakes and his tribike screeched to a halt, wheels tearing into the soft ground. "Nobody move," he commanded. The night air boiled with thick dust. Moans sounded over the open radio channel that linked all the C.A.D.S. suits. "Squad leaders, assess damages. Scan for mines, then get the injured to the Rhino immediately. But *be careful.*"

Immediately, everyone flicked to their assigned squad channels.

"MacLeish, what's your scan?" Sturgis said. "Do you register metal objects?"

"Negative," came the reply from inside the Rhino. "The damned mines must register as 'rocks' not mines. Somehow they fool the sensors."

"Billy," Sturgis ordered, "get up here fast. Use your jetpack and stick close to the road."

"Right away, sir!" Billy barely finished speaking before he was leaping up through the air like a space-age jack rabbit, bounding high over the abandoned cars and down again on the flame of his jetpack.

Sturgis was confounded. He turned on his G.I. mode and scanned the vicinity. The readout inside his helmet showed objects of all sorts of shapes and sizes—trees, bushes, even large rocks. Any of those blips for rocks might be mines instead. But why wasn't he getting a sensor reading for metal? Somehow these mines were camouflaged to foil sensors. *But how in the hell did they get here?* he asked himself again.

Then he had it. Of course! The mines had been *airdropped*. The Russian *could* have developed a new, disguised mine that could survive an airdrop, and then be triggered by sound or pressure on the ground. Not yet having the troop strength to occupy every part of the nation, the Soviets might want to pepper strategic locations with mines by air. And what more sensitive area than the main accesses to Orlando, where the Cubans were building their base?

"Billy," Sturgis said when the young man landed near him on the highway, "stay by the road and scout up ahead. I'm getting readings of dozens of rocklike objects that could all be mines."

Billy soared off on his jetpack and reported back in about ten minutes, "Affirmative on the mines, sir," he told Sturgis. "I did a high-magnification scan, and there are numerous round objects that are *all the same size*! I'd say we're facing a field of them about twenty miles long by fifteen miles wide, and we're smack in the middle of the width."

Sturgis swore. Even with high magnification, it would take them hours to pick their way out of trouble. They'd have a better chance if they waited for daylight. He ordered everyone to bed down for the night, right where they were.

When all reports were in, four C.A.D.S. Commandos were dead. A fifth, Jim Garrett, was critically wounded and had been taken to the Rhino. Sturgis summoned Dr. Smythe to see to the young man's wounds.

The prognosis was not good. Privately, Smythe told Sturgis he did not expect Garrett to last the night.

"Jesus," Sturgis said. "He's just a kid."

Smythe bunched his shoulders. "He took shrapnel in the abdomen, and his left hand is badly mangled. Frankly, I'm worried about gangrene setting in. I think the shrapnel is—tainted."

"Just do the best you can, Doc."

But when dawn came, Garrett was still struggling to stay alive. They would have to take him along and try to protect him in the coming battle. He could ride inside the Rhino.

Sturgis, Billy, and Tranh identified a mine and examined it from a safe distance. On casual glance, it looked like an innocuous rock, and showed up on the sensors as a form of granite or carbon, not metal. Day or night, they never would have known they were treading dangerous ground until a mine blew up.

"We'll have to get one of these to White Sands for analysis," said Sturgis. "This won't be the last time we run into these suckers. Let's hope the magicians back at Command can find a way to detect these things and modify the suit sensors."

There wasn't much left of the Commandos who'd hit the mines—just slabs and bits of flesh and bone, and metallic fragments of their suits and bikes. Picking their way through the deadly mines, their living teammates salvaged what they could of arms and supplies. The rest was abandoned. The shattered equipment would be of no value to any Russians or Cubans who passed through. As for the shattered bodies, they joined the other decaying remains around them.

Sturgis ordered the unit to about-face. "We'll retrace our steps and detour due east to get around this minefield. We'll take it slow until we're in the clear. MacLeish, if the Rhino gets to an impasse, stop and wait. We'll get the men out front and then figure out a way to detonate the mines."

The tribikes inched along, every man rigid in his seat, eyes darting back and forth between his screen readout and the ground ahead to dodge suspicious-looking lumps. But in an hour's time, in the clouded morning's light, all the men had managed to trace their way out of the deadly area. The Rhino was another story.

"I can't go any farther," Rossiter radioed Sturgis finally. "Too many blips on the screen. I don't know how the Rhino managed to make it this far into the mines, unless I rolled over some duds. Medic's in the back with Garrett," he added. "He's bad off, Commander. Smythe gave him some more morphine."

"Stay put, Rossiter," Sturgis commanded. "We're coming back for you guys."

Sturgis took Fuentes, Dixon, and two others and went back into the danger zone on foot. The only way to get the Rhino to safety was to blast out a path. He hated to waste the ammunition, but there was no alternative. Sturgis raised his right arm and loosed a burst of 9mm machine-gun fire, detonating one of the mines from fifty yards.

The men worked methodically, protected by their suits as long as they didn't step directly on a mine. Finally the Rhino was free to roll through the cratered area.

Once past the minefield, Sturgis changed plans. He was gambling that the airdropped mines were used in place of enemy troops or surveillance. "How much can we push the Rhino?" he asked Rossiter. Forty miles an hour was the battle wagon's usual cruising speed; sixty miles per hour, the maximum, could cause bearing burnout.

"I'm good for sixty," came Rossiter's answer.

Sturgis opened the throttle and kicked his tribike into a higher gear. "Then, let's detour west," he said. Engines roared and the Commando unit bounced and tore through the countryside, away from the hell zone.

They hadn't gone five miles when they heard the distinct sounds of a Jeep and several old panel trucks.

"Everybody freeze!" said Sturgis. "Defensive mode A!"

Fenton cut the Rhino engine. They were in a good position, on a hill in the cover of an extensive orchard of somewhat-denuded trees. Sturgis took Billy with him to the edge of the orchard to take a look at what was coming. To his annoyance, Peppercorn, who Fenton had suit-lifted out of the Rhino, was rolling alongside them, his wheels making a whirring noise. Sturgis decided it couldn't be heard over the noise of the approaching vehicles. But he motioned Peppercorn to hang back.

They reached a spot where they could get a good look at a dirt-and-gravel country road. "Telescopic mode," Sturgis commanded, and his computer function responded instantly, magnifying his vision tenfold. Now he could see clearly who was coming.

"Maximum audio," he said. The responding roar was almost painful in his ears, even though the vehicles were almost a mile off.

The men in the Jeep looked like Americans. They wore plaid shirts and cowboy hats, and were joking and conversing in English with a definite Georgia drawl.

"It's okay," said Sturgis. He was wondering whether the group of men below were just gutsy, or foolish, or whether they had hard intelligence that the Reds weren't around. They certainly were advertising their presence.

Peppercorn squinted into the distance. Suddenly his face lit up with recognition. "Yahoo!" he screeched. Before Sturgis could react, he recklessly propelled himself down the steep hill to the road.

"Jefferson, McCreedy—it's me, you sons of bitches—Peppercorn!"

The Jeep and trucks slammed to a halt and a group

of rough-looking men piled out and gathered around Peppercorn, hollering and slapping his shoulders in greetings. With his macro hearing, Sturgis heard the crusty old man explaining he had "some weird-suited buddies up on the ridge." Peppercorn waved madly at him and Billy to come down, but Sturgis waited a few moments until he figured the newcomers wouldn't be too startled by their armored appearance.

The man named McCreedy, tall and bull-necked with a ruddy face and veined nose, saluted poorly when Sturgis and Billy joined the group. "We dropped by your swamp base and had some nice hospitality from your womenfolk," he said, smiling. "Then we decided to catch up to Peppercorn and you fellas. We knew about this old farmer's road—ain't on no map."

Sturgis nodded. "I wish we'd known about the road."

"Well," McCreedy went on, looking uncertain, "we'd like to lend a hand, that is, if you'd let us. Can you use forty mean, sons-o-bitch Revengers out for Russky blood?"

"With me as your leader, he can," Peppercorn blustered out. "Me and Colonel Sturgis here are old friends."

Sturgis sized up the group. These boys looked as tough as they come, and Peppercorn had already vouched for their fighting ability. He sure could use extra help.

"It's dangerous as hell," he growled. "But the more the merrier. You're welcome to join the party."

Orlando was as bleak and desolate as every city the C.A.D.S. Commandos had encountered since the Russian's one-day nuclear strike. It was a ghost town of empty buildings and skeletons. Orlando had scored a direct hit from a small neutron warhead. People had died by the hundreds or thousands wherever they stood when the bomb hit. The buildings were undamaged for the most part, though some looked warped and melted, like butter left in the sun. The rad count was down enough to allow humans limited exposure.

Sturgis halted his men on the outskirts of town and took an advance party out towards Disney World, where the Cubans had holed up to establish their base. From an orange orchard hill three miles distant, the huge amusement park—twice the size of the island of Manhattan—looked ready to embrace throngs of smiling, happy guests. As they drew closer, they saw the empty avenues and the still rides. The vast parking lot was empty—any Cuban vehicles were somewhere else.

The saddest sight of all was the once-glorious Cinderella's Castle, the symbol to all America that fairy-tale dreams could come true. Its proud spires were bent and fused together. The whole structure had the same melted look as other neutron-blasted buildings in Orlando.

Were Sturgis's unit and the Revengers to do battle for the survival of the nation here, in the land of dreams?

Under the cover of the grove of orange trees, which

bore dry powderlike fruit that dissolved when touched, Sturgis continued to scan for enemy activity. Suddenly a gate to the park proper at the far end of the immense lot opened. "Telescopic mode, twenty power," he intoned. Immediately his visor displayed a close-up of the moving vehicle—an old Russian transport truck. The truck leaving the gate had a canvas-covered back, but that was no obstacle to his radar and his G.I. mode. In a short while Sturgis knew what was in the truck: Two men up front, and a whole bunch of flattened wooden crates. The crates had probably carried heavy equipment—or weapons—in.

Sturgis and his men withdrew a mile, then Sturgis took a chance and jetted a hundred feet into the air and used a variety of modes of vision to scan over the wall, all on maximum telescopic mode. By the time his fifty-second skyhook job was done, he knew there were lots of Cubans inside, and lots of weapons. There would be a battle. And the odds would be awesome.

But so were the C.A.D.S. suits.

CHAPTER SEVEN

"It's weird," said Dixon as the scouting party—Dixon, Fuentes, and the colonel—moved back toward the main C.A.D.S. force in twenty-foot-long strides. "Why Disney World, of all places? Why not the airport, for a Cuban base? I don't see anything that makes an amusement park ideal for a base."

"Disney World *is* the ideal base," responded Sturgis. "It's got lots of hidden nooks and crannies. And Epcot Center in particular has an underground labyrinth—miles of tunnels, service areas, and vacuum sewage tubes. The tunnels are a perfect, rad-free hideout for the enemy."

"That's where we hit them?"

"Right. In the tunnels. We'll do a 'search and eliminate,' locate any guards stationed aboveground at tunnel entrances. Depending on the situation, we'll either have to take care of the guards, or we'll find unguarded tunnels to make our entry. Our computers will calculate the best approach."

"But how will we know which tunnels lead where?"

"Thanks to the Revengers, we've got more maps," said Sturgis. "McCreedy and Aspen used to work at

Epcot. They did the laundry, and worked in one of the underground service areas. All the employees had maps that laid out all the tunnels and rooms—otherwise, they would have gotten lost.

"McCreedy saved the maps as souvenirs, and luckily, he had them in his truck all this time—in the glove compartment."

Ten minutes later, Sturgis and his six officers leaned over those maps. The maps were gaily colored drawings with a big, smiling Mickey Mouse at the top. Blue, red, yellow, and green veins crisscrossed each other, interspersed with workrooms. Disney World had always promised adventure to everyone who came. Now the place would offer the C.A.D.S. Commandos the ultimate adventure—battle.

Despite himself, bittersweet memories flooded Sturgis. He recalled the trip he and Robin had taken once to Disney World, shortly after they were married. It had been a fun, spur-of-the-moment trip, and they had felt like kids again, laughing their way through the rides. They screamed their way through every turn and plummet on Thunder Mountain Railroad, and when every monster popped out at them in the Haunted Mansion. And at Seven Seas Lagoon . . . he could still hear the beautiful, lilting classical music that had accompanied the mechanical frolic of neon dolphins.

Robin and Sturgis had been in absolute awe at the size of the place. Disney World, some thirty miles south of Orlando, covered an incredible 28,000 acres. Epcot Center alone was 260 acres. Along with thousands of other equally awe-stricken visitors, they rode the monorails and marveled at the magic of the place.

Robin was particularly taken with River Country, a recreation of an old-fashioned swimming hole, just like the one she used to swim in as a kid in Virginia.

But it was Epcot Center that impressed them the most, literally boggling their minds. The "Experimental Prototype Community of Tomorrow" was filled with the wizardry of computers and high tech. In Future World, they took the dizzying, spiraling, eighteen-story ride to the top of Spaceship Earth, the giant geosphere that symbolized Epcot. They saw three-dimensional movies created by computer-generated graphics, and rode sun-powered cars. They saw animated dolls sing. And they were filled with patriotic pride in the theme of the World of Motion: *"It's fun to be free."* Everything in Epcot glorified America's technological innovation and leadership.

Walt Disney envisioned Epcot as a "living blueprint" of the future. But in one big atomic flash, both the present and the future had changed irrevocably. Now Epcot and the rest of Disney World belonged to some dim and distant past. They were part of a world that no longer existed—and might never exist again, Sturgis thought grimly. If only they all could get on a time-travel train and really go back to the days before the bombs fell.

Sturgis didn't like to think about what might have been. All he had to deal with was reality, and reality was not pleasant. He squared his shoulders. He had the attack strategy all planned in his head. Even with the maps to guide them, it would be touch and go all the way.

Sturgis carefully delineated the parameters of his attack plan, using a short stick to point to the various places they would breach the security walls without firepower, with just the metal-tearing, concrete-busting power of the C.A.D.S. fists.

Juan Cordova, general of the Fidel Castro Brigade, sat back in the plush comfort of his new headquarters below Epcot Center. His first priority in taking charge of Epcot had been to refit one of the subterranean service rooms as his personal quarters. His soldiers had snatched bits and pieces of exhibits aboveground, building him a luxurious setting.

A short, wiry man with curly dark hair and an unkempt, scraggly beard, he put his feet up on the Lucite table and lit a fat Havana cigar. A sweet aroma filled the air, and the filter generator kicked on to draw in the smoke. Now that Cordova's own needs were taken care of, he could address the development of the base itself, and the establishment of an impenetrable security system. His troops were three hundred strong, and from here, they would spread out and fulfill the annexation of Florida to Cuba.

"Florida should have belonged to us in the first place," he muttered, reflecting on the Spanish ancestry both places shared. He tugged at his ratty beard as he spoke. "Ricardo!"

His fatigue-uniformed assistant, scrawling away in a logbook at a table on the opposite side of the room, jumped. "Yes, General Cordova?"

"What reports do we have on the unfortunate Americans above us in their radiation-scorched homes?"

"Scattered resistance by vigilante groups," said Ricardo, shuffling through his pile of papers. He pulled out a sheet and glanced it over. "But it's weakening. Mostly, they seem to be destroying each other over women and food."

Cordova gave a low laugh. "Taking Florida will be as easy as killing chickens in a barnyard. Once we have Florida, we will bargain with Moscow for Georgia and Alabama. And after Georgia and Alabama . . ." He puffed on his cigar contentedly.

"About the security system, sir?" ventured Ricardo.

Cordova frowned. "Yes, what about it?" He was annoyed at having his daydream punctured.

"There are delays, sir. Communications says it won't be up and running for a few days yet. They're working—what do the Yankees call them?—they're working the 'bugs' out. And they keep finding new tunnel entrances that must be guarded."

Cordova harrumphed, waving the concern away with an impatient gesture. "No matter. From what you say, we have nothing to worry about anyway. The Americans are shattered—they are no threat to us."

The general puffed on his cigar and admired his furnishings. He had no idea how costly his decision to build his quarters first, at the expense of his security system, would be.

On the hill overlooking Epcot Center, the C.A.D.S. team and the Revenger irregulars gathered, ninety in all.

Sturgis said, "C.A.D.S. goes in five teams, each to a separate tunnel entrance; the forty Revengers stay on the surface. I don't know where the Cubans' command center is, but I would place it near the center of the complex, so I assume they did, too. I'm not sure that it's there, so report on any possible location you find—any of the big storage areas are a likely bet. Maintain radio silence until we have made enough noise that you are sure they know we're coming, then keep in touch with me and your team members by radio.

"Unit One—Roberto leads. Two—Fenton; Three is mine; Four is led by Tranh. Five—Billy's; Six, it's Pepp's Revengers as rear guard. They will stay on the surface, secure the areas outside the tunnels—okay, Peppercorn?"

Peppercorn winked. "Right. I'm going to safeguard your rear ends." He fingered his electric controls. "This wheelchair does all right." He pulled up his blanket and showed the twin 9mm machine-gun snouts on either side of his crippled legs. "Fully loaded."

Sturgis snapped his helmet shut. There was no stopping Peppercorn.

The C.A.D.S. attack on the Cuban-infested Epcot Center was swift and furious at 0500 hours. Leaving their tribikes and the Rhino hidden behind in deserted Adventureland, the forty-nine Tech Commandos rushed Epcot Center, spreading out in teams to assigned tunnel entrances that were unguarded, followed by Revengers. They relied on their computer grids and screens since silence on the radio was crucial for the surprise.

Mickey Rossiter was distraught at being left behind in the Rhino. He was aching to see action, but Sturgis had put Rossiter in charge of the Rhino war-wagon this time. Fenton MacLeish, the usual driver of the Rhino, would be more valuable putting his antiterrorist training to use against the Cubans in the underground maze clad in a suit.

As soon as they were belowground, the troopers were at a disadvantage. The tunnels simply hadn't been built to accommodate seven-foot, two-hundred-pound combat armor. The tight fit drastically cut their maneuverability. Sturgis hoped the Cubans had no tricks up their sleeves that would turn the tunnels into a cemetery for the Americans.

The Commandos advanced, heading for, he hoped, the nerve center of the underground network of tunnels and rooms. Sturgis could almost feel the saddened spirit of old man Disney himself leading the way. The tunnels were lit with fluorescent light—evidently the Cubans had successfully restored the generator.

"Mode red," Sturgis said. Immediately his suit computer flashed a grid map inside his helmet showing the location of all C.A.D.S. troopers. The red-colored dots moved jerkily toward the middle of the grid.

"G.I. mode." Instantly the readout changed. The grid map vanished and was replaced by another multicolored map.

Holy shit! Sturgis looked again at the readout. It indicated the presence of more than three hundred human beings. Discounting his own men, that meant there were about twice as many Cubans as they expected! Well, it was too late now to do anything differently. Sturgis charged ahead, his heavy feet crunching against the cement.

The first Cuban he found was bent over a piece of sewage pump machinery in one of the service areas, with tools spread out on the floor around him. As Sturgis burst into the workroom, the man looked up to see a giant, black-suited monster bearing down on him—perhaps he thought one of Disney's own creations had run amok. He opened his mouth to shriek, but Sturgis closed a powerful hand around his throat and crushed his windpipe in one squeeze. The Cuban gasped his final, rattled breath, and his eyes bulged until they threatened to pop out of their sockets.

"That's for all the free men you bastards killed in your own country." Sturgis flung the limp body away from him, cracking it into a wall so hard that the skull split open and brain matter mushroomed out. The body slid to the floor in a bloody trail down the cement. "That's for you and all your stinking *compadres*. . . ."

In another tunnel, Fenton MacLeish led his team into a nastier greeting from the Fidel Castro Brigade. Six Cubans, armed with Russian Kalashnikovs, were crossing tunnels on their way somewhere they'd never get to. At the sight of the seven-foot C.A.D.S. men, they opened fire. The bullets bounced harmlessly off the suits. Fenton grinned wickedly as he closed in on them. The six kept on spraying bullets, backing away, horrified looks on their faces, shouting at each other in Spanish. With a flick of his wrist, MacLeish finished them off with a stream of 9mm slugs. "Too good for you bloody bastards," he snarled as the bodies jerked and fell. Fenton's team stepped over the tangled bodies. . . .

Tranh Van Noc felt almost as though he were back in the Cong's tunnels in Vietnam. This was just a different kind of tunnel, but his instinct was to crouch and move stealthily, something that was impossible in the C.A.D.S. armor.

He spotted one of the enemy far ahead and quickened his pace. Too bad the tunnels didn't have room enough for using the jetpacks, he thought, as he picked up his stride.

His quarry saw him coming and took off in the opposite direction. The man tried evasive action by dodging down an intersecting tunnel. Van Noc smiled. "Got to get this guy," he said softly to himself as he tracked his target with his computerized sensors.

The Cuban turned into another tunnel. Tranh heard a heavy, metallic clang. When he turned into the tunnel himself, he was confronted by a solid steel door that had slid into place across the way.

"So you think that's going to stop me, eh?" he said with amusement. He raised his left arm. "E-ball!"

A crackling, white-hot electro-ball shot out from under his arm. His visor changed instantly to a protective dark tint to shield his eyes from the blinding light. The heat was intense, but he didn't feel a thing inside his armor.

In nanoseconds, the E-ball punched a hole clean through the two-inch-thick steel. With his steel hands, Tranh widened the hole with a quick ripping apart of the remaining metal. He stepped through. His quarry had been momentarily confident of being protected by the door. Now he stood stupidly with a look of amazement on his face. He turned to run, but

Tranh cut him down with a quick burst of submachine-gun fire that set the man's back ablaze. Tranh continued forward, a perfect killing machine. . . .

As usual, Billy The Kid Dixon found the oddest place to fight. He got lost and wound up in an exhibit at ground level. It was the China Pavilion, filled with antiques, Buddhas, a thousand oriental wonders lit eerily by the helmet low-strobe. Someone tripped a switch accidentally. The 360-degree movie screen circling the room came to motion and sound. The startled C.A.D.S. men were sailing down the Yangtze River rapids!

And there, silhouetted against the screen, by the door, were two Cubans, who had snuck up there to hide. Billy smiled, fired on submachine-gun mode. They tumbled onto each other in a heap, like trophy ducks piled up on the first day of hunting. Bright red blood poured out from the wounds, mingling and pooling on the glazed brick floor. The silent Buddhas stared on impassively. The movie died.

Dixon stepped over the bodies and motioned to the C.A.D.S. men behind him. "Come on, guys, the party's just starting!" He let out a rebel yell. Let those Commie Cubans hear him now. "Back down the ramp we came up. . . ."

In a tunnel that the projected grid map showed should intersect Sturgis's path, Roberto ran as fast as he could. He wondered when he was going to meet the enemy. So far, the tunnel had been empty, and he had ordered all but one of his team to search out adjoining tunnels. Now he and Steve Rains clumped along single file as fast as they could in the cramped space.

Roberto's G.I. mode flashed the warning of nearby enemy personnel. "Vector zero," he shouted to Rains in warning. "What the hell—?" Vector zero was straight overhead!

A sudden impact of minor force from above caused Fuentes little alarm. Was it falling plaster? He twisted to see two Cubans crawling frantically over Rains, who'd been hit from above. The Cubans craftily had been clinging to pipes that ran along the ceiling of the tunnel, and had dropped onto Rains with monkey wrenches. The Cubans were screaming at the top of their lungs. The one on Rains was trying to cut through his C.A.D.S. armor's electrical wiring with a survival knife, digging into the space between helmet and suit.

Fuentes struggled to get one of his arms into a firing position. He was wedged almost crosswise in the narrow tunnel, and for the first time ever, cursed a blue streak at the bulkiness of his protective armor.

Rains also was having trouble. "The servomechanisms, he cut . . ." he gasped into his comonlink. "Can't . . ." He tried to reach behind him to grab the Cuban's arms or legs.

The survival knife broke against the tough armor, sending the Cuban into a wilder frenzy. He whipped out a hand grenade, pulled the pin, and jammed it into Rains's armpit.

"Rapid fire!" shouted Fuentes as he raised his left arm toward the struggling men. A spray of submachine-gun bullets caught the Cuban and sent him flying backward. Bullets chewed holes in the tunnel walls and ricocheted back and forth. The pings reverberated for a few seconds—then the grenade blew with a deafening roar.

The blast threw Fuentes backward. When he looked up, all he saw were chunks of concrete raining down on him, pounding against his suit, burying him in rubble and dust until nothing was visible. "Rains?" he asked. Silence.

The explosion reverberated throughout the entire underground maze of tunnels. "Mode red, split!" yelled Sturgis. "G.I. mode!" His helmet readout split into two screens, revealing everyone's position and identifying a huge blockage in one of the tunnels. The maps indicated the presence of two C.A.D.S. men in the middle of the blockage.

"Analysis!"

The names of Fuentes and Rains appeared on the cave-readout. CONCLUSION: GRENADE EXPLOSION AND CAVE–IN OF SURROUNDING MATERIAL.

Sturgis opened his commlink. He didn't care if the Cubans picked up the transmission—the surprise was long over now. "Fuentes! Rains! Report in!"

He got no answer. "Fuentes," he repeated.

At last a groggy voice came back over the com-link. "Sturge—" It was Fuentes. "Sturge, we got hit by a grenade. Damn suicidal fucker. I can't move. Can't see anything. Must be a ton of concrete on top of me."

"What about Rains?"

"Rains? Yeah, he's dead. Took a direct-contact hit. I think he's under the same pile of shit I am."

"What about you?"

"I'm all right as far as I know. Except I can't even move a pinky. I'm flat on my ass. The servomechanism is knocked out—I don't know how long the suit will hold."

"Are the jetpacks working? Can you blast your way out?"

"Negative, Colonel. Judging from my position, I'd say the packs are crushed."

"Colonel." Fenton MacLeish's voice broke in over the commlink. "I'm not far from the cave-in. Request permission to assist Fuentes."

"Like hell, MacLeish," Roberto answered. His voice was stronger. "I can last awhile. Get in and finish the fuckers, right, Commander?"

Before Sturgis could speak, a tremor shook the underground web of tunnels and rooms. It felt like an earthquake, but Sturgis knew what it was: the tunnel fight was getting hot—more than submachine-gun fire. That meant more tunnels were in danger of collapsing. They'd have to work fast before they were all buried alive.

Sturgis gritted his teeth. "Permission denied, MacLeish. Carry on with your orders. Roberto, hang in there. We'll get to you as soon as we can."

"Go get 'em, Sturge," Fuentes said. "Sock one for me." Another tremor shook the ground.

Sturgis opened the commlink to the Rhino. "Rossiter, bring her in!"

Mickey Rossiter had been monitoring the attack with the sensors on board the Rhino. He watched the progress, the blips of light change and disappear, and witnessed the cave-in that took Rains's life and trapped Fuentes. He sprang to the controls and revved the engines of the mighty oval battlewagon. He had expected Sturgis to call in the Rhino as reinforcement in the last stages of the battle, when the colonel expected to flush the remaining Cubans topside. But things were going wrong early in the game.

"Come on, baby!" he said as he gunned the machine to its top speed of sixty miles per hour. He'd worry about burned-out bearings from overdrive later.

The Rhino tore through the deserted Epcot grounds, barreling over empty snack stands and big pots of long-withered flowers, crushing everything in its path into sticks.

General Juan Cordova heard the distant boom of the grenade going off and felt shock tremors pass through the walls of his newly appointed quarters. At the same time, one of his men burst in the room in a state of absolute panic.

"General! We're under attack! An invasion!"

"Calm down, Garcia," ordered Cordova, leaping to his feet. He tried to shake the panic that gripped his own gut. He shot a sideways glance at Ricardo and saw his assistant's face frozen in a weird half-smile. Terrified!

"Americans! They've got robots, huge black things," jabbered Garcia. "They're all over the place, coming through the tunnels. They've blown up Tunnel Ten!"

"Dios." Cordova's hand went to his stomach. Giant black robots? That could mean only one thing—the legendary Blacksuit Commandos. Cordova had heard about them and their phenomenal strengths and capabilities. Supposedly they were invincible, far

superior to the Russians' high-tech Graysuits. But Cordova had never seen one of these commandos—and he had no desire to see one, especially now, trapped dozens of feet below the ground. The general liked to talk about courage, but the yellow stripe down his own back was a mile wide.

Garcia slammed a magazine into his pistol. "We are all going to die," he moaned. "I know it!"

"Shut up, you sniveling coward," growled Cordova. "Get out of my sight before I shoot you myself. No one in the Fidel Castro Brigade talks like that!"

The frightened Garcia was only too happy to flee.

Cordova turned to Ricardo. "Contact our Russian compadres, Channel 36–I." The assistant started to say something about how escape was more important, then clamped his jaws shut. It would not be in his best interests to anger Cordova. He got on the shortwave and began transmitting to Charleston.

Cordova took a Kalashnikov off the rack on the wall and checked the clip.

A fresh wave of tremors, much stronger than the previous ones, shook the tunnels. Overhead, fluorescent lamps swung crazily. Cracks opened in the curved walls, and dust fell on the Cubans' heads.

"Make sure everyone hears," said Cordova. "My orders are the same to all units. Communicate to them—to stop the Americans at all costs!"

Sturgis and his men pressed on, ignoring the quakes and the widening cracks in the tunnels. They *had* to pierce the nerve center of the Cuban base and destroy its leaders. They had to *find* that nerve center, though, and no one had reported coming on any Cubans over lieutenant's rank.

As they pushed in, they met wave after wave of armed Cubans trying to get out. The tunnels filled with the smoke of gunfire, and echoed with the screams of dying men. In some tunnels, the smoke was so thick it obscured vision, and C.A.D.S. troopers had to switch to their infrared strobes to pick out and mow down the enemy. With their puny combat weapons and antiquated Russian rifles, the Cubans were no match for the C.A.D.S. firepower, and they died by the score.

But still more enemy soldiers came on, screaming like wild men with hate in their eyes. The Americans kept up a steady fire, and when ammunition began running low, wondered how many more Cubans there possibly could be.

When MacLeish ran out of 9mm submachine-gun bullets, he switched to darts. In a quick draw, he nailed three Cubans. One dart pierced a man through his left eye. Blood gushed out, spraying MacLeish's black armor with red. The enemy soldier was dead before he fell.

They were coming so fast at him now that MacLeish barely had time to think. All he could do was react. He kept firing and firing until his darts were gone. "Bloody hell," he growled, switching to his liquid-plastic fire. He would avoid using E-balls, which could collapse the tunnels. He aimed his LPF, and two Cubans burst into flames. They were incinerated in moments, their last bullets richocheting off his suit.

Desperate Cubans no longer hesitated to hurl their

grenades, despite the dangers of cave-ins.

The fantastically brave unarmored Revengers took their toll of those Cubans who thought they'd escape to the surface.

Sturgis was the first to find and break through to General Cordova's command center, only to find it abandoned. A cigar still burned in an ashtray, a general's jacket hung on a wall. Damn! With a yell, he raised his powerful arm and smashed it across the communications console, destroying both the internal intercom system and the base's link with the outside world.

The lights abruptly went out, plunging the Epcot underworld into darkness. Pandemonium erupted everywhere. The C.A.D.S. troopers turned on their high-beam helmet lights. Then the overhead lights flickered back on as an emergency generator took over.

A rumble shook the tunnel system again, and Sturgis realized *this place could go down any minute*! Rossiter's voice crackled over his commlink. "They're starting to come topside, Colonel. Heading for the lagoon. Shall I waste them?"

"Save your ammo for now, Rossiter. Let the Revengers get 'em, but back them up if necessary." Sturgis got on the commlink to address all the C.A.D.S. Commandos. "Four men—E Squad—to vector seven immediately to rescue Fuentes. The rest of you, get out and head for the lagoon." Then he found the escape ladder and headed up. He hoped he could find the officer he had just missed visiting.

Peppercorn Williams, his age-spotted hands working the electric controls of his wheelchair, roared down the narrow length of the monorail track overlooking the crystal pyramids of the "Journey into Imagination" exhibit. His doughty warriors were scattered elsewhere in high vantage points and strategic hiding places. They all waited for the rats to flee the sinking ships—the Communist Cubans were coming out of those tunnels in an attempt to escape. Peppercorn had gotten five already.

With expert, high-powered-rifle fire, the Revengers had already picked off the two dozen or so who had run from the various tunnel entrances. But that was only a small number of the enemy troops who were still below. Williams was getting tired of waiting. He wanted more action.

"Wahoo!" screeched Peppercorn. His sharp eyes had spotted another "rat," slipping out of a tunnel. The Cuban came blasting out like a rocket. "Look at that sucker—scared as a jack rabbit," he crowed as he shot his wheelchair along the ramp and positioned it in front of the monorail train, which long ago had stopped in the track. Another Revenger fired and the man in front of him went down with bits of flesh flying.

"Revenge! Revenge!" hollered Peppercorn, practically hopping out of his wheelchair. His legs were getting hot from the heat of his double death dealers.

Several pops sounded, and the monorail train car windows near Peppercorn shattered. One of the Revengers nearby staggered back, his chest burst open in a mass of raw flesh and spurting blood. Peppercorn screamed in fury. He grabbed his binoculars and searched the buildings below his vantage point.

More pops sounded as more glass shattered. "Get down, Boss!" shouted one of his men, trying to push the old man out of sight.

Peppercorn shoved the Revenger back. "Stop that, boy, I know what I'm doing! No one's going to kill Peppercorn Williams! Now, get away from me and find the damn fool who's got the nerve to shoot at us!"

A burst of machine-gun fire came from a nearby Revenger submachine-gun nest. The American looked toward the monorail and gave the victory sign, thumbs up, after his Cuban target fell.

"That's the way, boys!" Williams shouted gleefully. "That's the way!" He rocked in his wheelchair like a man possessed by Tasmanian devils. "Revenge for America! Land of the free! Wahoooooo!"

MacLeish, Dixon, and two other C.A.D.S. troopers converged in the smashed tunnel that pinned Fuentes beneath a pile of rubble. Even with their power arms, it would take too long to manually remove the pieces of concrete.

Fenton quickly gauged the thickness of the debris with a computer analysis. "We can't waste any time," he said hurriedly. "It's got to take an E-ball."

"But Fenton, an E-ball could blast clear through to him, maybe even through *him*," protested Dixon.

"The concrete on top of him should absorb it," the Britisher said with finality. "Stand back." As the others obeyed, Fenton raised his right arm and gauged the angle. Then he fired an E-ball so that it would blast off one side of the pile.

The two-inch-thick explosive did the trick. It blasted apart the pile, sending hundred-pound pieces flying in all directions. The C.A.D.S. men dodged the fallout, then scrambled to pull away the remaining hunks and free Fuentes.

"It's about time," complained Fuentes in mock anger when he opened his helmet. "I'm missing all the fighting!"

"There's still plenty of it topside," Dixon said. "Come on!"

Even though the sky was overcast, the daylight was still almost blinding after the semidarkness of the tunnels. Special filters on the C.A.D.S. helmets helped the troopers adjust quickly. Sturgis still hadn't found his elusive general when he joined the others up on top. The scene that greeted them in the lagoon was one of pure horror.

The disoriented Cubans were plunging headlong into the stagnant, slimy waters like panicked lemming going over a cliff. The Revengers were closing in around them, picking them off as they thrashed about in the water. The Cubans fired indiscriminantly into the air around them. Revengers unlucky enough to be too close and in the open fell.

Sturgis caught a flash of commander's stripes among the Cubans. So that's where he is! He took aim and loosed an E-ball. It was a lot of firepower to waste on a single target, but Sturgis wanted to make sure his general was obliterated. And in one searing flash, he was—along with ten others.

Nearby, Rossiter had wheeled the Rhino into position. He swung around one of his six Redeye missiles and launched it. Moments later, the entire lagoon went up in a mushroom blast of water and mud. When the waves settled, nothing moved. Pieces of guts and limbs bobbed to the surface.

Sturgis was about to congratulate his troops and take stock of casualties when his G.I. mode lit up with a warning, and his Probability of Destruction mode flashed .8495. In the same instant, he saw the reasons for the warning sweep ominously into view low in the sky.

"Russian White Wolf choppers," Sturgis shouted. "Dozens of them! Take cover!"

CHAPTER EIGHT

The swarm of Russian choppers filled the sky within moments, bearing down at full speed upon the scattering C.A.D.S. troopers and Revengers. The combined roar of their engines was deafening. They rained death upon the streets of Disney World, the strafing machine-gun fire and bombs blasting whatever they hit into oblivion, Cubans or Americans.

Sturgis's computer analysis identified more than thirty of the lethal White Wolves, each armed with .50 caliber machine guns and several of the newest and most deadly Russian air-to-ground antiarmor missiles, the Zircon-10s, and two had three-foot antitank missiles, the Havocs. They were C.A.D.S. destroyers.

This was no routine Soviet patrol that had just happened to encounter trouble at Epcot Center, the C.A.D.S. leader realized. This was an organized attack mission. The Cubans must have sent out a call for help before their damned central communications center was destroyed. He should have reached it faster.

This was not the first time the C.A.D.S. troopers

had faced many Red choppers. The last time the Americans and Soviets fought like this, the Americans had wiped out the choppers. But this time, the odds didn't look so good. They faced more than double the number of choppers, buzzing and turning on dimes, coming at them from all sides at once. And Sturgis had less men to counter them with.

In the command chopper, Lt. Col. Alexei Kulikov raised a clenched fist in exultation at the scene below. This time these miserable, troublesome "Tech Commandos" or "Blacksuits" in their fancy spacesuits would be put out of action *permanently*. General Juan Cordova's call for help couldn't have come at a better moment. Kulikov's unit was the nearest to Disney World, and he and his well-armed attack choppers had raced to the scene at three hundred kilometers per hour from Macon, Georgia.

For Kulikov, this was his big chance to get noticed by the top brass. He would be certain to get a promotion for removing this ugly thorn in the side of the conquering Red Army. Perhaps even a general's ribbon awaited him. He would not make the same clumsy mistakes of that stupid Major Pitrochev, who had needlessly sacrificed fourteen White Wolves to this American unit not long ago.

"Your time's up, American imperialists," gloated Kulikov. "I know how to deal with you!"

On the ground, Sturgis was trying to spread out soldiers. "Get yourselves cover, only come out to shoot! Use your computers to calculate where the target's going to *be*, not where it is. Lock on and fire those E-balls at the choppers with the big Havocs slung under them. Get the others later."

Sturgis picked out an oncoming chopper and waited for it to get in range. He saw its machine guns smoke. Bullets pelted his suit without harming him. He raised his right arm and sent off an E-ball. In a white flash, the missile incinerated the Russian chopper's nose. The craft careened crazily through the air and crashed into the side of the huge geosphere of Spaceship Earth.

Sturgis scanned around. Other C.A.D.S. men were picking up the trick, letting their computers track the swiftly moving bigger choppers and then firing up E-balls. But the White Wolves were lightning fast in their dodging, and some seemed to outfox the tracking. Many of the E-ball missiles whizzed harmlessly past their targets. Sturgis realized with a sickening feeling that the enemy had some sort of E-ball deflectors. They'd have to smash the attack without the electrically-charged death-dealers.

Sturgis had to get his men back to their tribikes, which were armed with surface-to-air missiles—if the Zircon and Havoc missiles didn't get *them* first. He saw one C.A.D.S. trooper go up in a blast and hit the ground in a crushing impact. He knew there was no point in checking for injuries—there wasn't enough left of the man after the Havoc hit to justify a look-see.

The Revengers were sorely outgunned in the fray. They had neither the protective armor of the C.A.D.S. suits, nor the high-tech firepower. They had only their ragtag collection of hunting rifles and a few automatic advance combat rifles they'd scavenged from a U.S. Army depot. They were dressed in street clothes and hunting fatigues.

What they lacked in firepower, they made up in courage, racing out into the open as the White Wolves streaked down, pumping their bullets into them. Sturgis realized they were sacrificing their lives to distract the Red fire. He ordered his men to run from cover to cover out toward the hill and their camouflaged bikes.

In the Rhino, Rossiter was madly spinning the turrets of his twin .40 caliber machine guns and surface-to-air missile rack, sending back returning fire against the screaming helicopters. One missile found its mark and exploded a White Wolf in a ball of orange flame. The chopper disintegrated in midair. Blackened pieces of metal and dismembered bodies plummeted into the lagoon to join the other carnage. Rossiter hit another enemy craft with intense, accurate machine-gun fire. Bullet holes blossomed in the fuselage and windows. The engine choked to a halt. For a terrible few seconds, the chopper seemed suspended in air. Then it pointed nose down and whistled to a crashing destruction.

"Sturge," Rossiter hollered over the commlink, "I can take a lot of them down, or I can get on the remote control and send the tribikes down on automatic to meet you guys. What do you want?"

"Tribikes, pal—we'll do the best we can to meet them halfway," said Sturgis.

In a few moments, Rossiter had the Rhino moving in a random zigzag pattern among the withered orange trees on the hill, while he activated the tribikes' remote-control panels. He was acutely aware that one well-placed antitank missile and the Rhino would be shrapnel. If the Rhino were destroyed, it would be spell disaster for the C.A.D.S. unit. Without the Rhino, the C.A.D.S. men would have no way of recharging the atomic batteries of their suits.

Thank God the tribikes were hidden, Sturgis thought. He hoped the hiding place hadn't been discovered by the Russians and that it hadn't taken a stray missile hit.

Rossiter got the tribikes going slowly down the hill, riderless. The C.A.D.S. men yelled a cheer the likes of which Sturgis had never heard as they rushed out and mounted the mighty things. Their movements were masked by clouds of black smoke emitted from their suits—the smoke units installed at White Sands after the last mission.

From above, Kulikov watched the billowing smoke. Damn! What was going on? "Fire at random," he ordered, "—into the smoke!"

But the tribikes and their riders already were in the cover of the skeletal orange groves. Now the tribikes' racks of surface-to-air missiles sailed death into the sky.

Despite the dizzying speed of the Russian attack, the C.A.D.S. troopers were far from defeated. More than a dozen Red choppers suddenly lit up the sky like supernovae. E-balls sizzled through the air. But the remaining choppers still had more ammo than the Americans.

Billy Dixon fired off his last Hawk missile. "Shit, this is too slow for me, Sturge!" he hollered into his commlink. "There's only one way to get 'em!" He let out a war whoop and launched into the air on his jetpacks.

The liftoff took him straight to eye-level with a low-flying Russian chopper pilot, who stared at him in open-mouthed amazement. Billy gave himself a short jetblast to the side. He reached out and made a power-assisted punch clean through the metal of the helicopter. He put his hand in the hole and yanked with all his might. The side of the copter sheared off in a jagged tear. Billy enlarged his hole.

He threw the metal down and hauled himself aboard. "Okay, fuckers, say your prayers!"

The Russian machine gunner was barely out of his seat before Billy's flaming liquid plastic turned him into a human inferno. Dixon hosed the screaming crew in the hellish liquid, and he jetted out of the chopper as it spun burning to the ground.

Below, the C.A.D.S. troopers shouted in triumph. Those who still had enough juice left in their jetpacks followed Billy's example, jump-jetting to the enemy craft to battle them right in the sky. The Russian pilots tried evasive moves, but the packs enabled the C.A.D.S. troopers to move nimbly.

Fenton MacLeish shot up with a roar and punched his way onto a White Wolf. The Russian crew jumped on him, trying to push him out, but they were no match for the supersuit. MacLeish grabbed two by the scruff of the neck like puppies and tossed them howling to their deaths. He stormed the pilot and copilot, who were desperately trying to fly their craft and defend themselves at the same time, firing Tukarov 7.2mm guns.

"Let me show you the *only* way to fly," growled MacLeish. He hooked his powerful arms around their throats and hauled them backward through the helicopter. They thrashed and screamed to no avail.

MacLeish heaved them out the hole torn in the side.

Kulikov couldn't believe his eyes as the battle turned against him. This was impossible! The White Wolf was the most savage attack helicopter in the Soviet military, and these were armed with the latest weapons. How could these Americans, even in their armor, take them apart like this? And those three-wheeled vehicles flitting about among the trees! What were they?

In the center of the grove, Kulikov spotted a truck of some sort, bristling with guns. No, it was a tank, with wheels, not treads.

"Destroy their tank," he ordered his crew. "They conceal and defend it so furiously—it must be part of their life line. Vector five. Now!"

Sturgis sighted in on Kulikov's copter bearing down on the Rhino. He was low on ammo. He didn't know if he had the battery power to jump high enough to reach the flying death machine. He tracked the flight path by computer, and when his readout flashed that it was at its lowest point in the trajectory, he blasted himself up into the air.

He could see he wasn't going to make it. He fired the jets again, straining and reaching as far as he could. With a grunt, he grabbed the tail just as the gunner fired an antitank missile at the Rhino. The copter jerked, and the missile went off course to explode harmlessly in an empty stretch of trees.

Sturgis used a last boost from his jets and flipped on top of the chopper. The pilot tried to shake him off by bouncing the copter up and down at high speed and turning in circles. Sturgis, prone on his belly, hung onto the roof with all the strength he could muster out of his suit. The C.A.D.S. armor gloves gripped the copter in an indentation in the metal. The rotors missed Sturgis's helmet by only inches.

He hammered away at the metal, punching his right fist through it. Then he grabbed the opening. The metal tore away like eggshell.

Sturgis used his remaining machine-gun bullets on the two gunners, cutting them into pieces. He headed for the cockpit and shot the pilot through the head with a dart as the other turned and emptied his pistol harmlessly at Sturgis.

"Well, what do we have here?" he said, when he saw Kulikov's command stripes. "The leader of the pack! Mister, you picked the wrong fight!"

Kulikov flung his arms in the air in surrender, but Sturgis only laughed. "Come on, asshole, you don't think I'm gonna fall for that. You guys don't know the meaning the word 'surrender.' And you sure as hell don't know the meaning of the word 'mercy'!"

Sturgis seized Kulikov by the throat. His windpipe was crushed instantly and his eyes rolled up. He gurgled frantically for a few seconds and died. Sturgis pulled him up out of his seat and dumped him on the floor. The copter was dipping out of control, engines stalling. Sturgis grabbed the stick. He couldn't read the Cyrillic markings, but he reasoned that Russian helicopters had to operate basically the same as American ones. He succeeded in righting the White Wolf and pulling it out of its stall. Using his G.I. mode, he found the automatic pilot and switched it on.

He turned to the Russian gunner. "Okay, fucker.

Your turn."

The Russian pleaded for his life with tears streaming down his face. Sturgis ignored the waterworks. He couldn't understand the language, and was glad he couldn't. He picked up the Red and stuffed him up through the opening torn in the roof. "You've got lots to think about while you're outside," he snarled. "Enjoy the walk."

Sturgis returned to the cockpit and slid into the pilot's seat. He took the White Wolf off auto and tested the controls.

Only four Red choppers remained of the once-mighty force that had begun the attack on the C.A.D.S. force. One of them contained the Russian squad's second-in-command, Major Garganin. He was horrified at the beating his side was taking and was scared out of his wits. He was only twenty-two years old, and had planned on spending a few comfortable decades as a conquering hero in the new land. Why didn't Kulikov have enough sense to cut their losses and clear out? Now, where was his command ship?

Garganin saw Kulikov's copter flip-flop through the air, then right and steady itself. He asked for instructions over the radio and got nothing. That worried him even more. Then he saw the commander's White Wolf head after another Russian chopper, and figured it must be a retreat. Perhaps the commander's radio was out.

Garganin ordered his pilot to swing around and follow. He was shocked out of his senses when he saw Kulikov's chopper gun down one of his own craft with a single Havoc missile. The chopper burst into a ball of flames and fell.

Piloting the command ship, Sturgis didn't even blink before aiming his guns at another White Wolf. A Zircon heat-seeker shrieked through the air and smashed into its target.

Two down and two to go. This was going to be short work, thought Sturgis.

By this time, the two remaining Red choppers realized Kulikov's ship was under enemy command. One swooped in and sprayed machine-gun fire at Sturgis's copter. The 30mm slugs chewed up the metal, but ricocheted off the C.A.D.S. armor. "Try harder, guys," Sturgis said through clenched teeth. He smashed away the broken windshield.

He slammed the copter into a steep dive. The attacking copter followed. He pulled up abruptly and spun around, catching the other ship in its dive. He hit the firing button for a Zircon. Nothing happened—the bay was empty. He hit another button for a Havoc, and the missile sailed out, right on target. The White Wolf exploded with a mighty roar, its missile, launched too late, spinning wide of his ship.

Garganin witnessed the destruction of the last Russian chopper besides his and decided he would rather be a live coward than a dead failure. It would be only his word, anyway, about what really had taken place, and he would see to it that his crew backed up his story.

"Disengage!" he screamed. "Full speed!"

Garganin's White Wolf took off like a rocket, heading north away from Disney World. Sturgis opened the throttle and pursued the fleeing ship. He saw he had plenty of fuel, and he was prepared to follow these bastards as far as necessary to get them. His copter was out of missiles—but he banked on having enough machine-gun bullets to finish the job.

The helicopters sped through the gray, overcast sky at three hundred kilometers per hour. Garganin's heart was in his throat. He couldn't shake his pursuer. He certainly couldn't lead the enemy back to his base. What else could he do?—Fly in circles until one of them ran out of fuel? Just hope the pursuer never got close enough to fire on him?

No, the Russian decided out of desperation. I must become the attacker again, not the target. It's my only chance.

"Give me those controls!" he said, pushing the pilot out of his seat. He swung the copter around sharply to the right, turning back on Sturgis with machine guns blasting.

Sturgis pulled up in a steep ascent and then dropped, answering with his own machine guns. The two White Wolves dodged and wove through the air in a dance of death.

"Track!" Sturgis commanded his suit computer. The readout in his helmet was dim and blurry, barely readable. "Track!" he said again, but there was no improvement in the image. The battery that powered his suit was damaged. Even his backup cell pack was drained. Suddenly he noticed he was losing his flexibility as well—the joints of his suit were stiffening. He didn't have much longer before he froze up completely. Damn!

He saw Garganin's ship come at him again, guns spitting. "It's either you or me," he said softly. "Maybe it's gonna be both of us." He turned his copter into the path of the oncoming White Wolf, opening up his landing gear. They headed straight for each other. Sturgis girded himself for a head-on collision. There were worse ways to die, and there *was* a method to his madness.

Sturgis pulled up. His landing gear smashed into the rotor of the other chopper and broke into pieces, Sturgis's craft groaning as it lurched sickeningly—but stayed up. He jerked his ship to the left and watched as the other chopper nose-dived to earth, its rotor shattered.

He watched the fiery impact, then slowed his ship, fixed coordinates back to Disney World, and put it on automatic pilot. He landed amidst cheers after radioing ahead that he had gotten the last attacker. His landing was rough, for without landing gear he had to set the ship down on its undercarriage. But any landing is a good landing, he thought.

"It's about time someone got here," groused Peppercorn.

Billy and Tranh exchanged lopsided smiles as Peppercorn glared fiercely at them. "If you boys were under my command, you'd step-to a lot more smartly."

The two C.A.D.S. Commandos picked their way through the rubble that had once been Disney's monorail. Most of the train lay in a twisted heap of scrap metal below, a bizarre coffin for a number of brave Revengers.

The front car, which Peppercorn had ensconced himself in, was half on the track and half hanging over the side of the elevated rail. The blast from the Russian missile had thrown the leader of the Revengers backward, turning over his wheelchair. Due to his paralyzed legs, he'd been unable to extricate himself. He had lain helplessly, staring up at the ceiling, arms twitching, listening to the monorail car creak and groan as it hung over the track.

"Are you hurt?" asked Tranh before pulling the old man up. They didn't want to complicate injuries by moving him.

"No, I'm not hurt," fussed Peppercorn, grabbing for their leverage. "But Jack is." He pointed toward a severely damaged part of the car where one of his Revengers had crouched to snipe at Cubans.

Billy followed his point. "Jack's dead," he said simply, once he had walked over to check. "His head's gone."

Peppercorn's wrinkled lips set in a thin line. For a fleeting moment, the fierce look in his eyes softened. Then he snorted. "Let's not be all day about it," he fumed, reaching up his arms to be lifted. "There's work to be done. Just pry that damned wheel loose, boy!"

All over Epcot, the exhausted C.A.D.S. troopers and Revengers were pulling themselves together, treating wounds and assessing the damages. All around them were horrid reminders of the death and destruction that had taken place. Bodies were everywhere. Some were whole and some were in shreds and pieces, looking like carcasses of meat savaged by wild animals. Dead Cubans floated in the lagoon like bloated fish.

Wreckages of the Russian choppers were scattered

everywhere, too. Fires burned and raged where some of the copters crashed. The American survivors managed to extinguish the biggest fires, but small ones still sent inky smoke into the polluted sky. The smell of high-octane aviation fuel mixed with the stench of burning flesh and burning buildings. Smoke rose from the fires below.

Blood was splashed and dotted on nearly every building and all over the ground. It was as though someone had sent a giant drum of red paint into the air on a rocket, and exploded it over the area.

At least, the earth had ceased to shake and rumble with the threat of more collapsing tunnels below. Perhaps the underground had stabilized. Taking no chances on further shifts, MacLeish dispatched a crew to search all tunnels for any survivors.

At the Rhino, Rossiter was busy recharging the jet packs. The fighting had ended in the nick of time, for the men had expended ammo like it was inexhaustible. They needed to reload their arm braces with E-balls and submachine-gun cartridges. Some suits were wrecks.

Fuentes set his suit on self-destruct. The servomechanisms were damaged beyond repair from the cave-in. It was an ironclad rule that useless suits be destroyed, so that the Soviets could not find them and learn their technological secrets. Fuentes salvaged a suit from a fallen comrade. The poor bastard had died from a heart attack, according to his readouts.

Dr. Harry Smythe, the C.A.D.S. unit's medic, had his hands full at a makeshift treatment center for the wounded. The Revengers had suffered over fifty percent casualties. Nothing could be done for the ones who needed extensive surgery, but still lived.

Sturgis had gotten out of his suit. He wanted to walk around like a human being, see with human eyes, feel the cool wind on his skin. Leaving his suit at the chopper, he made straight for the Rhino himself and climbed down in. Mickey gave him a status report. No enemies taken captive. Sturgis didn't ask for elaboration on the latter. It was a rule that the C.A.D.S. unit not be burdened with prisoners. Any enemy soldiers unlucky enough to survive a battle never survived the clean-up afterward. America was no longer a country kind to its visitors.

"How are the tribikes?" Sturgis asked, once seated alongside Rossiter.

"Just three knocked out," Rossiter reported.

Sturgis blew out a sigh of relief. "Thank God," he said. The tribikes were their only means of transportation. He drew out a pack of Marlboro Lights from the chest pocket of his shirt and put one between his teeth and lit it. He sucked the smoke in deep, feeling the heat in his lungs, savoring the nicotine.

"We've got to move on as soon as possible," he said at length. "Russky reinforcements may be coming."

"We're getting the suits juiced up as fast as we can."

Suddenly Sturgis noticed that a makeshift cot in the Rhino was empty. It had been occupied by Jim Garrett, the trooper who had taken a Soviet mine blast on the journey to Disney World. Sturgis remembered the young man had not been expected to live.

"What happened to Garrett?"

Rossiter shook his head in wonderment. "He was a strong guy. He steered the Rhino while I fired at the

Red choppers. Bled to death doing it. A hero."

Sturgis clamped his teeth around the cigarette and drew in another breath. One more good man down—one of the best. "Greater love hath no man than he who lays down his life for another . . ." he whispered.

"Sturge," Rossiter exclaimed, "you're bleeding!"

Sturgis looked down at his own body and was surprised to see his clothing encrusted with dried blood. A gash in his shoulder blade was still slowly oozing. He didn't feel any pain. He'd had no awareness of being injured.

He shrugged. "If it hasn't stopped me by now, it's not going to," he said gruffly.

Sturgis left the Rhino in time to see Boss Peppercorn Williams roll up in his powered wheelchair. One of the wheels was slightly bent, and it created a lopsided wobble. Peppercorn was oblivious to it, and steered his chair like a captain piloting a mighty ship. Under other circumstances, the feisty old man would have looked hilarious. But nobody was laughing today.

"Colonel," he greeted Sturgis. "What do you plan to do with that chopper you set down?"

"E-ball it." Sturgis ground out his butt beneath his heel. "There's no point in letting the Russkies get it back."

"Well, give it to me. I want it."

Sturgis stared down at Peppercorn, his blue eyes hard. "What the hell for, Pepp?" He respected the old man and was grateful for the Revengers' assistance. But sometimes he thought Peppercorn got carried away in war fantasies, and he was in no mood to play games.

"To ferry out the wounded, Colonel. Some of my men can use it to fly the injured back to our headquarters."

"Are you crazy? You want to take that Russian crate into Soviet-controlled airspace, all the way back to Georgia? You'd be shot down! One radio contact, and they'd know you weren't one of them."

"It's the only way," argued Peppercorn. "Otherwise, what are we going to do? We certainly can't leave the wounded here. And we can't take them along, either. Some of them shouldn't be moved, and those that can move won't go very fast."

Sturgis rubbed the grizzle of whiskers on his chin. "We've got the Rhino and a few extra tribikes. The bikes will run on autopilot and can be accommodated to those who need to lie down. I ordered a doctor to come with the airdrop we're expecting in the Okefenokee. And good medical supplies. The wounded would—"

"They'd be better off at our base, Colonel."

"Sorry, Pepp, I can't allow it."

"Sturgis, I know it's a risk, but I'm willing to gamble. Let me get those boys back home, where they can get the proper attention and get back on their feet as fast as possible. I'll take any of your men who are also badly hurt. It will take hours, not days, by chopper."

Sturgis considered Peppercorn's proposal. Pirating a Red chopper ran a grave risk of being either shot out of the sky or forced down to capture. "No," he said sadly. "If you're captured, you would all be tortured for information. And some would crack.

The best thing is for the wounded to go back with me."

Sturgis saw the unhappy look on Peppercorn's face, and the rebuttal already forming on his lips. He didn't want to discuss the matter anymore. It was settled as far as he was concerned. "Excuse me," he said. It came out curtly but he didn't apologize. He turned on his heel and headed toward the area where the wounded were being collected.

"Dixon," he called out. "What's the report on the wounded and the dead?"

"Not good, Colonel, but it could have been worse. We lost eight of our own men and twelve Revengers. Looks like we've got another twenty wounded. At least five are in serious condition and might not make it. One of the Revengers used to be a preacher—the medic's got him giving last rites." Then Dixon's face turned grimmer. He pointed to the end of a row of wounded, where a badly damaged C.A.D.S. suit lay in a burned and melted lump.

"See that?" said Billy. "There's a man still inside that suit. He's literally fused in. Must have been some kind of high-voltage short circuit. I don't know how in the hell we're going to get him out. If we cut away the suit, we're going to take his skin with it."

"Has he had morphine?"

Dixon nodded. "We haven't got enough, though. Smythe is stretching it as far as he can."

"Give this man whatever he needs, even if someone else has to do without. Do the best you can to get him out. We can't leave him in his suit."

"Yes, sir."

"What else, Dixon?"

"That's the worst. The others that are critical have suffered severe blood loss. Some have missing limbs. Other than that, we've got some broken bones and the usual bullet and shrapnel wounds."

"Have Smythe set the breaks and get the wounded ready for transport as soon as possible. The extra tribikes can ferry some of the wounded on autopilot, controlled by another rider."

"Right, sir. We found some carts on the grounds here. If they've got gas and can be started, we can use them, too."

"Then get on it. We've got to set some charges, blow this place up, and get the hell out of here before the Russians get wind of what we did here!"

CHAPTER NINE

First there was a muted boom. Then the rumble started deep and low, like the growl of an animal on the defensive, then crescendoed to a roar. The ground heaved and shook. Cracks split the concrete and grew into crevices, tearing the buildings of Epcot Center wall from wall.

The international restaurants and souvenir shops of Future World became piles of matchsticks. Glass in the crystal pyramids of the "Journey into Imagination" shattered as the pavilions imploded and sank. The geosphere Spaceship Earth, which looked like a giant, faceted golf ball rising high above Epcot, cracked like an egg and broke into pieces that crashed down atop the rubble of other buildings.

Then the ground itself began to sink as the underworld honeycomb of tunnels narrowed and collapsed. When the shaking finally stopped, most of Epcot had dropped into a shallow pit covered with the ruins of exhibit palaces.

Sturgis turned to Peppercorn Williams. "You have the deepest gratitude of myself and my men, Pepp, for your assistance. We couldn't have done it without the Revengers, and I'm sorry about your losses."

The Southern soldier shrugged, uncomfortable with the praise, yet there was pride in his pale blue eyes. "It was our duty, Colonel," he said thickly. "We'll be there whenever you need us. We've all got a long fight ahead.

"We'll be heading south, now, me and my men decided," Peppercorn added. "We're going to join up with some of our boys already down in the Everglades. Don't trust them sneaky Cubans. They're probably already sliding through those swamps like a bunch of hungry alligators. We got to stop them there, just like we did here."

"I wish we could return the favor and help you out," Sturgis said. "But we've got urgent business up in the north. The Soviets are turning the East Coast into a vast base."

"That's all right, Colonel. If we meet the Cubans in the Everglades, we'll be getting into some nasty swamp fighting. The swamp's going to be the death of those señors from the Caribbean. Got to slink and slip around like jungle guerrillas. We'll be using what you taught us here—and we know how to live off the land and find food supplies."

Sturgis smiled warmly. If only there were more men like Peppercorn Williams, brave and hearty and willing to go the distance for their country. America could use more like him, instead of traitorous, selfish dog packs of barbarians who were roaming the land, working for the enemy—*turncoat* Americans.

"You heading straight for Charleston, then?" asked Peppercorn, "—right after you go back to your swamp base?"

"No, we're staying for a while in the Okefenokee. We've got to refit and repair bikes and C.A.D.S. suits. Lick our wounds. Get orders from the President."

Peppercorn nodded. "I want to tell you, Sturgis—your unit sure is the best hope for America. I'll miss fighting alongside you, boy. Here," he said, lifting a flask from under the blanket across his lap. "A healthy swig of white lightning is as good a good-bye as I can make."

Sturgis took a drink. "Good-bye." He reached out and grasped Peppercorn's liverspotted, blue-veined hand in a firm handshake. "Till next time."

Peppercorn tried to remain the stern soldier he envisioned himself as being. But the expression on his face was unmistakably affectionate, the way a resolute uncle looks upon a favorite nephew with approval.

After Epcot, everyone without exception was anxious to get back "home" and relax. Their base's primitive conditions loomed in the minds of the troopers as the height of luxury and comfort as they drove back.

The old slave ruins in the Okefenokee didn't offer much comfort, really—a collection of crumbling, roofless foundations that looked more like an archaeological dig than a secret special-forces base. The ruins offered no plumbing, indoor or outdoor, and no fresh water. Drinking water was taken from a trickle of a stream and chemically purified. The tech soldiers had constructed a crude outhouse so that waste didn't become a problem. Polyvinyl tarps were strung across the roofless shacks to protect them against the elements. Beds consisted of sleeping rolls spread out on piles of palm fronds—not exactly Sealy Posturepedics, but better than the hard ground.

Still, the old slave ruins were home, the only home the C.A.D.S. troopers had away from White Sands headquarters. Real homes, the ones they all knew and cherished before the war, were no more. "Refuge Island" was now "Home Sweet Home," as some of the soldiers dubbed it with bittersweet affection.

When they arrived—escorted the final leg of the journey through the swamp channels by a fan boat full of waving swamp women—the C.A.D.S. men were greeted with surprise. Refuge Island was not as they had left it.

"I must be seeing things," muttered Billy. "Sturge, have we died and gone to heaven?"

"I don't believe it, either," Sturgis said. He halted the tribike column just on the edge of the village.

Everything looked different. The aged huts still stood, but their walls were patched and rebuilt with mud. The polyvinyl tarps were gone, replaced by neat, thick thatch roofs made from woven palm fronds and sawgrass. The footpaths between the huts were cleared of debris and vegetation. The whole place was swept and picked clean—it definitely had a woman's touch.

But what was far better were the swamp women themselves. They didn't look like dirty warriors anymore. Instead, they were scrubbed clean and had put brilliant-hued tropical flowers in their long hair. The animal hides they had stitched together for clothing accentuated their ample female charms. Without exception, they were beautiful young women—definitely a sight for sore soldier eyes. They stood in a knot, anxious to greet their homecoming soldiers.

"I don't know about you, Sturge," said Dixon, "but that's for me!"

"Welcome back, Colonel." A tall, statuesque woman with flashing green eyes stepped forward. It was Dieter, the queen leader of the swamp women. She moved with regal catlike grace. Her once-tangled auburn hair was brushed smoothly to her waist. She was tan and slinky, and her allure wasn't lost on Sturgis. He discovered he wasn't as tired as he had thought.

"Congratulations on your victory," Dieter said in her soft Southern accent. "Everything here is secure. We had no trouble while you were gone. As you can see"—she swept out her arm to indicate the renovated shacks—"we made a few changes. I'm sure you'll find them to your liking." Dieter smiled. "Why don't you all get out of that armor? You'll feel much better after you've cleaned up. We've prepared a meal—fresh catfish and heron, and some healthy oranges. We'll make you as comfortable as possible."

Sturgis had the women help take care of the wounded first, setting them down as comfortably as possible in the new quarters. Some of the fourteen women stayed in the huts to comfort and care for them.

Sturgis gave the long-awaited order to the men to fall out and relax.

Dieter held out her hand to Sturgis. Behind her, smiling swamp women came forward to greet the

C.A.D.S. troopers. Billy zeroed in on a luscious-looking brunette who had the longest legs and the scantiest outfit of resewn pieces of cloth.

"Come with me, Colonel," Dieter said. "I have something to show you." Her eyes of flecked gold flashed.

Out of his suit, Sturgis began feeling his aches and pains for the first time. I'd give anything for a hot bath and a massage right now, he thought.

As they entered the hut that was his personal quarters, Sturgis wrinkled his nose. "What's that smell?"

The swamp queen laughed. "Perfume! Wild orchids and lilies, crushed a bit to bring out the scent. No offense, Dean, but you men could smell a little better." She wrinkled her nose prettily. Alone with him, away from her new "tribe," she seemed demure, like a well-refined Southern woman—which is probably what she had been before Macocco's swampers had kidnapped her.

Sturgis looked down at his coveralls. They were almost stiff with grime and dried sweat. His own skin felt like elephant hide. He wasn't aware of how badly he smelled—his nostrils had long since gotten used to it. But he was certain that in more civilized times, he would empty out a room of people in nothing flat.

"You're absolutely right," he said sheepishly. His dirt-streaked face broke into a grin. "I don't see myself as smelling like a lady's lingerie drawer, however."

She scowled in mock disapproval. "That's just for the air, honey." Her lapse into a Southern belle-ism—*honey*—made her blush self-consciously. "Look," she continued hurriedly, "there's something else I want to show you."

For the first time, Sturgis noticed the tarpaulin that had once been his roof. It was hanging from the ceiling in a corner of the hut, forming a little stall. Dieter swept back the tarpaulin, her face glowing with pride.

Sturgis could hardly believe his eyes. It was a shower stall! A primitive one, but still the real thing. The shower head, where the water came out, consisted of a small, hollowed tree trunk. The opening was covered with woven dried swampgrass, which created an uneven, but effective, spray. The floor of the stall was gently sloped toward one wall of the hut, and another hollow tree trunk, slipped through a hole cut in the wall, acted as a drain.

"How on earth did you do this?" Sturgis examined the handiwork. It was sturdy, not a haphazard job.

"Never mind the details. One of us used to be a lady plumber. The hollowed trees are courtesy of Macocco's camp. We simply made use of what was available, Dean. It had to be done, otherwise you fellows were going to be unbearable to be around."

"You made more of these?"

She nodded. "Not every hut has one. There weren't enough materials. But there are enough showers to keep everyone clean. Of course, the commander had to have his own."

Sturgis worked the hand pump to get water flowing. It splashed on his head and down his shirt front, cool, refreshing—and fresh. "This is fresh water!" he exclaimed. "Where did you find it?"

Dieter looked triumphant. "We discovered and

tapped an underground spring. You won't have to purify that awful swamp water anymore. There's plenty of this water for drinking and bathing."

Sturgis regarded her with frank admiration. Not long ago, Dieter and her women had been ragged, downtrodden captives of post-nuke rapists and cannibals. They had come a long, conquering way. "You're wonderful," he said sincerely.

She blushed again and lowered her eyes, which made her look even more full of charm and coquetry. "You're the one who's wonderful," she said. "You saved my life." Impulsively, she put her arms around his neck and kissed him lightly on the lips.

Sturgis, who had been admiring the figure she cut in her skimpy animal pelt, suddenly was very much aware of her femininity—her tan skin, her full, rounded contours, the way her generous breasts pushed out from the taut hide. It was obvious she wore nothing beneath the hide. A hunger rose quickly within him, a hunger that erased his need for food and sleep, a hunger that left him breathless. How long since he had been with a woman? His hunger demanded to be sated, and, in the far corners of his mind, he knew it had nothing to do with his love for Robin.

He reached out to caress Dieter's face. Her skin was warm and soft, like satin on a summer's night. She raised her eyes to meet his, and he saw the same hunger flashing in their green depths. There was a sudden, electric tension between them.

Dieter luxuriated in the touch of his hand on her face. Then she lowered her eyes again self-consciously and turned away. "I'll wait for you outside," she said, unable to hide the reluctance in her voice. "Supper will be ready."

"Dieter." His voice was husky as he took hold of her hand and pulled her back to him. She offered no resistance. "Don't leave me now."

He saw hesitation cloud her features. Her eyes searched his for a long moment while she worked out something internally, and then her expression cleared. "Things are different since the war, aren't they?"

"Yes, they are."

He drew her closer, wanting her badly but still willing to let her go if she desired. He was not the type of man to force himself on a woman, but God, he wanted her.

"My upbringing says I should leave," she said.

"And what do you say?"

"That I should stay. You're an incredibly attractive man, Dean. I thought so from the moment I saw you." She pushed her hands up the hard muscles of his chest.

"Then stay," he said, "and accept it for what it is. Nothing more. If you can stand me, that is."

She giggled. "It's nothing a shower won't cure." She slipped her arms around his neck again and he embraced her, pressing her full against him. She was a tall woman, but against him she felt small and vulnerable, and oh, so delicious. He wanted *all* of her.

"Dean—" she started to say, but his lips were already halfway to hers, and he cut off her words. Her lush, full mouth opened to take his tongue, igniting a fire there was only one way to extinguish.

He felt for the rawhide thongs that fastened her

animal skin and deftly undid them. As the skin fell away, he sucked in his breath at the dazzling magnificence of her body. He caressed her firm breasts and she moaned with pleasure.

Dieter drew her lips away and allowed him to undress her. Then she unbuttoned his shirt and pushed it back. She ran her fingers through the light hair on his chest, and gingerly touched the bandages that strapped his shoulder. Then she was at his belt, opening his trousers, touching him in ways that intensified his desire so strongly he thought he would explode.

When they were both naked, he pulled her into the shower and drew the makeshift curtain. He worked the pump until the sparkling spring water cascaded over them, mixing with the sweat of passion. Gently he pushed Dieter against the wall and pressed his body against hers. For a few moments, heaven would be theirs.

They relaxed on Sturgis's bed on the floor, propping themselves up with cushions of palm fronds. The Coleman portable stove cast heat and a golden glow about the hut, and a comfortable silence enfolded them. Sturgis had one arm draped around her shoulder, and smoked a cigarette with his free hand. Dieter was somewhere far away, judging from the look in her eyes.

They had dressed and eaten, and Sturgis felt satiated. He was nearly whole again, he thought. He blew a series of smoke rings into the air above his head. If only the woman next to him were Robin, he *would* be whole again.

He wondered if Robin had sought solace in the arms of another man. It wasn't the first time the thought had crossed his mind. Once, the very thought alone would have driven him to a white fury, and he would have killed any man who laid a hand on her. But now, in such a gruesome post-nuke world, surrounded and threatened constantly by death, could he really deny two human beings a moment of pleasure and release? The same pleasure he took himself?

Still, it made him uncomfortable, and he preferred not to think about it.

Dieter stirred, as though picking up his thoughts. "I wish I knew where he was," she said, her eyes still focused on some distant place. "My husband."

Sturgis sensed the woman needed a sympathetic ear. She may be Dieter the Swamp Queen today, he thought, but in the past she was someone else with an entirely different life. She needs to deal with a past that no longer exists.

"Where is he?" he prompted.

"Daytona. I think. I don't know. I don't even know if the city is there anymore."

"It is," Sturgis said. He omitted saying that chances were that few, if any, of its residents were still alive. "Is that where you're from?"

Dieter warmed to the memories. "Yes. I was born and raised a Southern belle in the Peachtree State, and moved to Florida when I got married."

"Isn't Dieter an unusual name for a Southern gal?"

She nodded. "Dieter's my married last name, actually. My first name is Gloria. I just started using it—it sounds much stronger—since I was—" she hesitated at the recollection of bad memories—"taken by the ones you killed.

"We Southern women are taught to be strong but not show it. I guess it can't be that way any longer. Only the strong are going to survive." Dieter was silent for a moment. "I don't know if I'm strong enough for this new world."

"You *are* strong." Sturgis crushed out his cigarette.

"I got married when I was seventeen to Wayne," she went on. "He is—was—an insurance broker. He wasn't at all like you, not so handsome. You know Southern men, they look a little soft around the belly. Well, I didn't work. My whole life revolved around the country club and entertaining his clients. My biggest decision was what color nail polish to use. Can you imagine? But it was a good life. I loved Wayne. We were happy. It was so, so *perfect*. Why did *this* have to happen?" She buried her face in her hands.

Sturgis had wondered the same thing at least a thousand times. "No one knows," he said, giving her a little hug. "What is, is. Save your strength for living, Dieter."

She rested her head in the crook of his arm. "I was in Jacksonville visiting my sister when the war came," she said. "I tried to get back to Daytona. I was in a panic, running around with thousands of people. I couldn't get through on the highway, so I started walking. That's when I was captured by—" she choked at the thought of Macocco and his gang—"those horrible swampmen."

Sturgis steered her away from remembering too

much about the tortures she had endured at Macocco's hands. "Do you have any children?" It proved to be the wrong question, much to his dismay.

Dieter shook her head. "I was pregnant when I was captured," she said. Tears welled in her eyes. She started to sob. "I—lost it."

Feeling terrible, Sturgis hugged her closer. Her hot tears soaked into his shirt. "It's just as well, Dieter," he said. It came out gruffly and he tried to soften his voice. "A baby wouldn't survive here. And the radiation—it would have been born deformed."

She stabbed at her tears and tried to compose herself. "I suppose . . ." She sniffled and twisted to look at Sturgis. "Dean, do you suppose Wayne's still alive somewhere?"

"I don't know," he said. "Just believe that he is."

She seemed to take comfort in his words and was quiet for awhile. "What about you, Dean?" she spoke up. "Have you lost someone, too?"

Sturgis seldom talked much about Robin. He held her close to his heart, as though talking about her would somehow dissipate her memory. He answered Dieter's question hesitantly, and then found himself opening up, telling about Robin, their marriage and separation, and their reunion shortly before the war pulled them apart.

Dieter absorbed it all with great interest. "You must love her very much," she said.

Sturgis shifted his weight and dug into his shirt pocket. He busied himself with another cigarette. "I do."

"I'm sure you'll find her."

He grunted. He was starting to feel uncomfortable

again. Too many emotions on the table.

"Can I ask you a favor?" Dieter said.

"Of course."

"Will you stay with me and hold me tonight?"

"Yes," he said. Perhaps in the night they would reach out again to each other. It was something they both needed.

"Christ, Sturge! Get a load of this!"

Roberto Fuentes waved a sheaf of dirty papers in the air. They were blackened and gritty, almost stuck together in a wad, but they comprised invaluable documents—plans, maps, communiqeès, reports, and orders. The papers had been seized at the Cuban command center. The frightened Cubans had never thought to destroy their sensitive paperwork before they stumbled and tripped over each other to flee the terror of the C.A.D.S. men.

Even with Epcot rendered useless for any future military uses, the Americans had yet a prize of greater value: top-secret information that hopefully would reveal enemy activities throughout the occupied regions. Roberto had been assigned to translate the Spanish.

He spread the papers out in front of Sturgis as they sat at a rough-hewn, picnic-type table in the mottled sunlight of a warm, humid Florida afternoon. "Do you want the good news first, or the bad news?"

Sturgis leaned back and took a drag on his cigarette. He had nearly smoked his way through his share of the airdropped, rad-free cigarettes, but his dwindling supply didn't slow him down. As he eyed

Roberto, he shook his pack, already thinking about lighting another one up as soon as he stubbed out the one in his hand.

"Let's hear the bad news," he growled. "The good news probably isn't much better."

"The Russians have sent in crews to repair the Chesapeake Bay Bridge Tunnel up north in Virginia."

"That *is* bad news. Those bastards don't fix anything out of the goodness of their souls. They must plan to deploy troops."

"You got it—motorized units, tank and armored car divisions. According to these reports, when the repairs are done, the Soviets will head south from their center in Washington, D.C., and then spread west."

"Sounds like the Red version of Sherman's March to the Sea."

"Just about. The plan calls for a solid occupation line between Washington and Tallahassee. From there, they will spread west. The Cubans were supposed to assist the Russians by clearing the freeway south of the bridge, but I guess we fucked that up for them."

"Only temporarily. When the Cubans realize we wiped out their men at Epcot, they'll be looking for us like a swarm of mad-as-hell hornets to make sure it doesn't happen again." Sturgis frowned. "So what's the good news?"

For the answer, Fuentes unfolded and smoothed a large sheet on the table. It looked like a blueprint, and was charred around the edges from the Epcot battle. Holes were burned through the paper at various places.

The paper bore diagrams of repairs being made, including sections of the bridge and the highway north and south that were to be modified to accommodate the Soviet troop deployments. Over that, Fuentes laid a Rand-McNally roadmap, which the Cubans had marked to show the routes the Soviets planned to follow south. Points were marked along the way indicating where Cubans were supposed to check in and make sure the way was clear.

Sturgis whistled. "Dynamite!"

"Yeah, we have nearly all the details—dates, troop numbers, weaponry. The Russians are going to push west, and these papers say exactly where and by what routes, but not *when*.'"

Sturgis held up the maps and examined them closely. "That shouldn't be hard to get. If anyone's going to know the dates, Jeeters will. Are we monitoring for his broadcasts?"

"Around the clock," Fuentes assured him. "He hasn't been coming on at his regular times. Either the Soviets are getting wise to him, getting tired of him, or there are broadcasting problems."

"Let's hope he holds out as long as possible," Sturgis said. "He's the most important spy in America. Let me know the minute he comes on."

Fuentes and Sturgis were interrupted by Private Larry Trent, who entered the command hut and saluted smartly. "Beg your pardon, Colonel, sir. It's the medic, Smythe. He's dying."

"He's *what*?" roared Sturgis, leaping to his feet. He was stunned. "Jesus H. Christ! Where is he?"

The private took Sturgis at a fast jog-trot not to the large hut that served as sick bay, but to another hut that had been empty. On the way, Sturgis told himself over and over again that Smythe couldn't—mustn't—die. It was impossible! He'd come through the battle at Epcot with hardly a scratch.

Sturgis burst through the hut doorway to see Dieter and two of her women huddled over Smythe. He was prone on one of the medical folding cots, covered with a sheet and looking deathly pale. The sheet was soaked with sweat, and Smythe, his eyes closed, twitched and jerked.

"What's happened?" Sturgis demanded. Dieter motioned for him to stay back, but he ignored her and came to the bedside. "I said, what's happened?" He felt Smythe's forehead. His skin was burning up.

"His temperature is at least a hundred and three, probably higher," said Dieter. She pulled Sturgis into a corner and spoke in hushed tones. "Dr. Smythe is dying, Dean."

"I know—of *what*? It can't be radiation sickness—he's had no symptoms. Dammit, he was a perfectly healthy man when I saw him this morning!"

"He's got something that could be more dangerous than radiation poisoning," Dieter answered. "It's blackwater fever."

"What are you talking about?"

"It's a—a—fever. I saw it when I was in captivity. Some of the women died from it."

"Well, do something for him!"

Dieter shrugged in a helpless gesture. "I'm not sure we can. The fever comes on fast—in hours. The victim goes into a coma. And never comes out." She sighed. "It doesn't seem to be very contagious. Still, to be on the safe side, we've got him here instead of in sick bay, and it's why you should get out of here right away."

The full meaning of her words hit Sturgis like a bomb. Blackwater fever! It could be their deadliest enemy. It could do what the Russians and Cubans had failed to do—decimate them, wipe them out. He felt his stomach twist into knots. He leaned against the wall and ran his fingers through his hair.

"What about you? And them?" He nodded toward the other women, who were mopping Smythe's brow and arms with cool, damp cloths.

"We may be immune. The fever seems to strike on a random basis. All of us women were exposed, but only four of us got it and died. I don't know why it hits some and skips others."

"It could be any of a thousand reasons." Sturgis thought fast. There was no point in pulling out of the Okefenokee and relocating somewhere else. They all were probably exposed by now to whatever carried the fever—bugs, maybe. Their best shot would be to get some expert medical help fast from White Sands. And pray for the best.

He looked over at Smythe again. "Are you sure there's nothing that can be done to help him?"

"Just make him as comfortable as possible. They don't last long once the coma sets in."

Sturgis went back to the cot. One of the women stepped aside. He took Smythe's limp hand, and he was silent for a few seconds as he composed his thoughts. He flashed on the hard times they'd shared, and how much his men relied on the medic. "I don't know if you can hear me, Doc," he said in a gravelly voice that came from deep within his throat. "I just want to say thanks from the bottom of my heart for your service to your country above and beyond the call of duty. You saved a lot of lives, and we are forever grateful."

When Sturgis turned away, there was a lump in his throat.

He cleared it noisily and then regained his cool composure. He took Dieter outside. "I'm going to raise White Sands by Telos-link," he explained. "I want you to tell the docs there everything you know about blackwater fever."

After Sturgis informed White Sands about the fever outbreak, Science Adviser Gridley got on the link. Another airdrop would be made, with more C.A.D.S. troopers and one hundred satchel charges of plastic explosive type 0-11. The satchel charges would be a tremendous asset, Sturgis soon realized from Gridley's description. Each explosive satchel was designed for throwing and came with a handle. Each was covered with a new adhesive that made it stick wherever it landed. The charge was detonated by remote-control voice command. Neat, real neat. The drop also would include transphasor diodes the C.A.D.S. troopers so desperately needed to repair the blown fuses on their suits.

Sturgis got word while he talked on the radio that Smythe had died. He clung to a grim hope that no one else would come down with the fever until medical help arrived. The western docs had responded with alacrity. The airdrop, Science Adviser Gridley told Sturgis, would include an expert doctor familiar with tropical fevers.

Gridley signed off and was replaced by Van Patten, whom Sturgis was anxious to talk to concerning the liquid wave amplifier laser weapons.

"I know you've got pressing problems, Colonel," Van Patten said. "I hate to add to them, but be advised that we still can't send any LWAs—yet. We still haven't corrected all the defects."

Sturgis blew out his breath in exasperation. Damn! "When *will* they be fixed?" he snarled.

"The parts that would make our job easier are missing," Van Patten replied coolly. "We are doing the best we can. The Exrell Corporation, you know, never delivered last December."

Sturgis let loose a string of expletives. Damn that fucking bastard Pinky Ellis, the president of Exrell. He'd sold out to the Russians. Why, oh why hadn't he blasted the shit out of that fat pervert when he had the chance?

President Williamson himself next got on the satellite commlink. After Sturgis filled him in, the President asked Sturgis to mount an offensive against the Soviets at Chesapeake Bay. Sturgis agreed that there was no choice but to use the C.A.D.S. unit again.

Thirty-six hours later, the last of the patched-up American airdrop droned away in the distance. From the hatchway of the Rhino, Sturgis heard the shouts of the men as they gathered the supplies. He watched the forty-odd men who had dropped down on the isle in the C.A.D.S. suits head into the settlement. They were back up to near full strength.

"Sir!"

"Yes, Jackson?" Sturgis glanced up at the trooper

who stood in the doorway. Behind the overalled trooper was a C.A.D.S.-suited figure. The armor suit was shiny and clean. New.

"Your new doctor, sir." The soldier stood aside.

Sturgis rose. "Thank God," he muttered. But the person who strode in wearing a C.A.D.S. suit put the visor up and shook out her hair. She smiled.

"Sheila de Camp!" His eyes widened.

"*Doctor* de Camp," the woman answered frostily, her own blue eyes snapping at him. She shook her head to loosen her wavy brown hair, which had gotten flattened inside the helmet. "Psychoanalyst, P.C., M.D., and D.D.S."

Sturgis was in a steam. "Those fucking idiots! I said I needed a *medical* doctor. You're a psychologist, for crissakes."

"You don't need to swear a blue streak at me, Colonel. You got what you asked for. I may be practicing as a psychologist, but I am also a trained general practitioner."

Sturgis was not to be appeased easily. The last thing he needed was to have this brassy woman here giving him a hard time. He'd had a run-in with her before, in White Sands, over her hare-brained ideas about counseling his soldiers. They ended their dispute amicably—Sturgis won, of course—but as far as he was concerned, the front line was no place for her.

"You're going back," he said flatly. "I don't care if the entire air squadron has to return to pick you up."

Sheila de Camp stood her ground. "My orders are to join your unit. I'm here to help you."

"I don't give a damn what your orders are. I'm giving you new orders."

"Colonel, it would be a big mistake."

"Read my lips, de Camp: There is no place for you here." He took a breath and throttled down. "Sorry, but that's the way it is. We need a *fighting* doctor!"

De Camp arched an eyebrow. "Are you afraid of having a *woman* with you?"

He clenched his teeth. "You're dismissed, de Camp."

Sheila refused to budge. "There is no other doctor to send," she said quietly. "If you want a doctor at all, I'm it. And I've had one month's intensive C.A.D.S. training!"

Super, thought Sturgis. Great. He rubbed his neck and put his hands in his pockets. He looked at the ceiling and then at de Camp. Her blue eyes were soft and glowing, and she was smiling at him as though she, woman, could tame the beast within the man. It rankled him, but he had no choice but to accept her.

"I'm sorry, Dr. de Camp. Welcome. As soon as you stow your gear, you'll have to work right away on this swamp-fever problem. I'll have someone brief you when you're ready. Any questions?"

"Just a request, Colonel. Will you help me get out of this suit?"

Sturgis looked at her keenly. He could read between the lines as fast as any man. Sturgis motioned for a C.A.D.S. trooper to come over. "Soldier," he said. "Assist the doctor."

The red-on-white words, "Freedom Broadcasting Network, Hartstown, South Carolina," which announced the Reverend Jerry Jeff Jeeters show, flashed on the base's TV screen forty-five minutes later. The C.A.D.S. trooper who was monitoring the set scrambled to get Sturgis. Sheila de Camp insisted on tagging along.

"Just what we need," she said sarcastically as the grainy image of Jeeters materialized on the thirteen-inch, battery-powered Sony. "A holy-roller revival."

"Quiet," snapped Sturgis. To the trooper he said, "Are we taping this?"

"Yes, sir. I'm also taking notes."

Sturgis sat back in his chair and instinctively reached for a cigarette. Fuentes, Tranh, and Dixon entered one by one and sat down without a word.

"I advise you not to smoke, Colonel," chided de Camp. "It's bad for your health."

"I assure you, Doctor, when I want your opinion, I'll ask for it." Sturgis blew out a huge cloud of smoke. "World War Three made the Surgeon General's cancer warning a laugh, don't you think?"

On the screen, Jeeters was heating up his pitch, waving a Bible and screeching at the top of his voice.

"And I say now, dear Christians, get down on your *knees*, get down right this minute and thank the Lord and his son, Jesus Christ, for sending us the Soviets who will save us from sin and all the evils we have visited upon ourselves! They will save us from our greedy, empty lives! Yea, we shall be redeemed through our Soviet saviors!"

De Camp gasped. "Who is this traitor?"

"He's not a traitor," said Dixon. "He's a hero—probably the most patriotic guy in the country."

"I don't believe it. Listen to what he's saying!" Jeeters was ranting on in hysteria about evil America being saved by the glorious Soviet Union. "Praise God for the Russians!" he shouted.

"I thought I explained to you once before that the world isn't a neat black-and-white place," Sturgis said.

His men suppressed smiles. Sheila de Camp and Dean Sturgis were like the space-age version of an old nursery rhyme—the hydrogen dog and the cobalt cat, who blew each other up in a nuclear blast.

"I *know* the facts of life," shot back de Camp. "And I know what this man is—he's no patriot, he's a Red."

"Wrong, Doctor. Jeeters has the Commies fooled. They think he's their propaganda machine. What they don't know is, he passes intelligence to the resistance fighters by citing Bible verses. Now be quiet so we can get the message."

De Camp opened her mouth to reply, then clamped it shut. For the rest of the program, she sat mesmerized by the Jerry Jeff Jeeters Show.

CHAPTER TEN

Robin mopped the thick, rich gravy with the last bite of her country biscuit and popped it into her mouth. The dinner of venison stew and biscuits warmed her innards and took the edge off her fatigue, and the sadness that weighed on her heart from not being able to meet Dean. Next to her, Chris put down his plate with a satisfied sigh.

"This is a great welcome, Sally Ann," Robin said, forcing herself to sound bright. "We've haven't eaten like this since—why, since we left here weeks ago. As I recall, you cooked that last dinner, too."

"We're glad to have you both back again," Sally Ann said. "You've had a long trip, and a disappointing one—try not to think about much of anything."

Sally Ann stood and scooped up the plates. She wore her long brown hair tied back into a pony tail. Her jeans and faded denim shirt were covered with a cheery red gingham apron. Sitting here around the rough-hewn oak table, enjoying a country meal in the light of a Coleman lantern, almost made Robin forget the pain of not finding her husband, Dean Sturgis, at the rendezvous point. It was warm and cozy with these mountainfolk who were trying to fight back against Russian conquerors.

"I bet you could go for seconds," Sally Ann said, interrupting Robin's thoughts. "I know you couldn't have eaten much out there in the mountains. There isn't much left to eat that hasn't been hunted down or scared off."

Robin waved her back. "No, I couldn't. Really, Sally Ann, I'm stuffed. It was absolutely delicious, though."

"*I'll* have some more," piped up Chris. "I'm *still* famished." Robin looked at Chris and smiled. The weeks trekking through the Appalachians had done wonders for Chris's self-confidence. He was much more animated and outgoing than when she had first met him. There were burns on the right side of his face, but he was hardly self-conscious about the nuke-burn anymore. Chris had matured rapidly under Robin's subtle encouragement, and was learning that true beauty and worth radiated from within.

"Seconds for me, too," added Jeb, Sally Ann's husband, who was sitting at the head of the small table. While his wife refilled the bowls, Jeb leaned back in his chair and picked at his teeth with a sliver of wood. His wiry red hair had a coppery cast in the lantern light, and his big familiar nose seemed dignified, not too large, to Robin now.

He hooked a thumb through his suspenders. "Well, it's a damn shame you couldn't meet up with that fella of yours."

Robin's hazel eyes were full of sadness. "We waited at the campsite as long as possible. I left a note for him where I knew he'll find it."

"You've got to keep hoping he's still alive."

Robin nodded vigorously. "Dean's a survivor. I know he's still alive, and if it's the last thing we do, Jeb, we're going to get back together."

"That's a powerful lot of devotion."

Robin didn't answer. She was thinking of the last time she and Sturgis had been together. She remembered exactly the feel of the smooth, hard muscles of his chest, the way she felt so small and protected in the strength of his embrace, the perfect fit of their two bodies. Transcending that was the deep love they felt for each other, a love that had almost been allowed to die, but then had been rediscovered and rekindled with even greater intensity. Then the war had cruelly separated them. But their love would not be denied this time, no matter what. They would spend their last breath, if necessary, to be with each other again.

Patience, Robin, she thought. We'll make it.

"Here you go." Sally Ann delivered bowls full of steaming venison stew to Jeb and Chris, and set a fresh basket of biscuits in the middle. The savory aroma of the stew filled the little mountain cabin.

Chris dove into the biscuits, smearing one with honey and gobbling it down, and dunking another into the stew. Jeb's huge hand closed around a couple biscuits, and he alternated between bites of biscuit and gulps of stew.

Robin allowed Sally Ann to refill her stoneware mug with strong coffee.

"I said in my note I'd try to meet him again—he'll know the exact place and time—though I didn't spell it out, in case the notes were found."

Jeb, hunkered over his bowl, slurped and swallowed noisily. "Listen," he said after dispatching a whole biscuit chased by stew, "you might know something about this: we got word while you was gone about some U.S. Army "tech-commandos" fighting the Cubans down in Florida. These guys don't sound like nothing I ever heard of—they was wearing these black spacelike suits and driving these strange contraptions what looked like oversized tricycles. Sounded pretty wild, like science fiction to me, and I told Al the fella who saw it all must have been smoking something."

"Jeb," Sally Ann scolded. "You shouldn't be so skeptical. You know it's perfectly likely that the government could have some secret projects, maybe lots of them. The U.S. isn't finished yet."

"Yeah, well, this sounds pretty weird to me."

Robin, whose eyes were growing larger by the second, thought her heart would stop. She grabbed the edge of the table. "That's good," she exclaimed. "Maybe—just maybe—it's Dean's unit! Where were they? When? What happened?" She fairly jumped up and down in her chair.

"Whoa, slow down, gal. No reason to think it's your fella. It's a long shot that it would be. I heard the unit is called "Cads." That sound familiar, Robin?"

Robin drew in a great gulp of air to steady herself. Dean might be very, *very* close. She *had* heard the word before.

"Cads," she repeated. "C-A-D-S. It—sounds familiar." She didn't tell them that was the word she had heard Dean mutter in his sleep several nights in a row, before the nuclear war broke out—the word Dean had told her *never* to acknowledge hearing.

Jeb nodded slowly. "As I recall, you was sayin' earlier, when we first met, something about your man being involved in secret work for the government."

"It was secret, up until the war. Dean's a colonel in the Air Force. He was put in charge of this special unit that was so secret, I never knew when I'd see him, where he was, or what he did."

"I told you it was something like that, Jeb," said Sally Ann. She was looking at Robin with new admiration. "This man of yours must really be something."

"He is," broke in Chris proudly. He glanced sideways at Robin. "Well, I've never met him, but I already know he's terrific."

Robin reached across the table to touch Jeb's arm. "Jeb, you've got to tell me everything. What happened in Florida?"

Jeb scraped his bowl of the last of the stew. "Details are kinda sketchy, mind you. Wasn't that long ago, a week, maybe. Seems this space-age army went into Epcot Center—you know, Disney World down in Orlando—and blasted those fucker Cubans out of the base they were building 'neath the ground in all those tunnels. Some mountain boys we know of who call themselves the Revengers helped 'em out."

"And . . . ?" Robin was almost afraid to hear more, but she *had* to know.

Jeb screwed up his weathered face into a scowl. "I gather there was quite a few casualties. After they wiped up the Cubans, the Russians surprised 'em with an air attack." He looked down. "Sorry to tell you that . . ."

Robin jerked as though a dagger had stabbed her through the heart. She tried not to imagine Sturgis falling under the strafe of machine-gun bullets.

"Jeb," Sally Ann said harshly. "Look what you're doing to the poor thing." She got up and came around behind Robin and put her hands comfortingly on Robin's shoulders.

"That's all right, Sally Ann," Robin said. "I need to hear about it. Dean's still alive, I'm certain of it. I think I'd know somehow if anything ever happened to him." She looked at Jeb again. "Go on."

"Don't know much more, ma'am. I'm awful sorry. They got the Russians, too, then gathered up their wounded and left. They were last seen heading north inland, up towards the Okefenokee."

"Did you hear anything about Dean, or about anyone by name?"

Jeb shook his head. "There was just a bit of information, y'see. And I'm gettin' this third-hand as is." He reached into his trousers pocket and extracted a brown leather pouch, long stained from handling. He pulled out a hefty wad of chewing tobacco and inserted it between his cheek and tongue. It made him look like a squirrel.

"I'll be darned," he said to no one in particular, grinning. "Space-age fightin' men. Lordy, we sure can use 'em! I want to meet this Dean Sturgis myself."

"They can't be too far from here—Okefenokee's about a hundred miles," said Robin. There was an intense look in her eyes. "I've got to go south, see if I can find them!"

"Now wait a minute," Jeb said. "I'm not so sure

that's a wise idea."

"Why not?" asked Chris. "We do just fine, Robin and me. We can make it anywhere!"

"Boy, haven't you realized by now the woods are crawling with Russians and Cubans? We sight more and more of 'em every day—scouting parties, most of 'em, but well-armed and just itchin' to blow a few Yankee heads off."

"We can handle ourselves," Chris insisted.

"I know you're pretty handy with a knife, and Robin can shoot that lever Winchester as good as any mountain man. But we're talking serious weaponry here. They got some might evil-lookin' machine guns, and every one of 'em is strapped with enough rounds to take the Alamo single-handedly."

"Jeb's right, Robin," Sally Ann interjected. "It's getting more and more dangerous around these parts. So far, we've been able to avoid being discovered, or else the men have picked them off before they could report in about us. But we don't know how much longer our luck will hold out . . ." her voice trailed off.

"Besides," Jeb went on, "even if you did find him, you might complicate things without knowing it. He might be getting his men ready for another engagement—or you might even walk into the middle of a fight."

Sally Ann let go of Robin and started clearing off the table. "I'll fetch some more coffee," she said.

Robin sighed. She had to admit to herself that Jeb had a very good point. She had to think of more than herself and Dean. Duty to their country superseded that.

Jeb aimed a spit at a beat-up little pot in the corner of the cabin. It hit with a wet, sloppy sound. "Here's what I think you oughta do. Sit tight with us until it's time for your next rendezvous. I know it seems like a long time off, but it's not, really." He gave her a grin stained with brown tobacco juice. "We'll help the time go fast for you. There'll be plenty of work—and danger—for everyone."

"What kind of work?" asked Chris.

Jeb smiled coldly. "Me and the boys have decided to shift from defense to offense. How would you like to go huntin' Reds?"

Robin didn't hesitate. "Count us in, Jeb," she said firmly. "Chris and I will do whatever is necessary."

At that moment, Sally Ann laid down a huge pan filled with a scrumptious-looking concoction of peaches, sugar, and cinnamon under a flaky pastry. It was hot and smelled heavenly.

"Sally Ann makes the best peach cobbler in the South," said Jeb. "You better dig in, 'cause it won't last."

"Wow," said Chris, devouring the pan with his eyes. He had the typical insatiable appetite of a growing teenager. "But what are the rest of you going to eat?"

They all chuckled. Sally Ann began dishing the dessert out onto plates. "I'm afraid these are the last of the peaches. That's right, Jeb," she added, seeing disappointment cloud her husband's features. The new fruit that was appearing on the trees due to the local false spring was bad fruit—it looked healthy on the outside, but was rotten on the inside. "This might be the very last peach cobbler you'll see for a long time."

She put a plate in front of Robin. "But let's not think about that right now," Sally Ann said. "Let's enjoy, and when supper's done, I'll bet we can get Jeb to pick a few mountain tunes for us on that old guitar of his."

"What's that?" Robin hissed. "That movement—right over there." Robin crouched in a stand of poplar and sweet gum trees that were nearly smothered by emerald kudzu vines. The thick vines afforded good cover for her, Chris, Jeb, and three of Jeb's mountain men. They huddled, stock-still, listening to the sounds of the woods and the rush of the breeze through the warm Georgia air, waiting for the Reds.

Chris followed Robin's keen-eyed gaze. "I see it," he whispered. He watched the bushes not far ahead vibrate and rustle. "It's on two legs, not four. Whoever it is doesn't seem to care about being detected."

On a signal from Jeb, the mountain men fanned out soundlessly. The rustling and shaking was coming closer. Robin raised her lever Winchester and tracked the movement through her telescopic lens. Jeb slipped off to the right.

The top of a head popped into view through the bushes—a dark-haired head, and Robin almost squeezed off a shot. Suddenly Jeb shouted, "Hold your fire!" He charged into the brush. A high-pitched scream tore through the air. Jeb reappeared in moments, poking a fat and very frightened girl ahead of him with his rifle. She was covered with dirt and her clothes were torn practically to shreds. Her dark hair was stringy and greasy. She couldn't have been more than sixteen.

"Don't shoot," the girl was sobbing. "Don't shoot!"

Robin lowered her rifle, and she and Chris went forward. The other mountain men appeared, and they gathered in a circle around the cowering girl.

"Lookit here," said Jeb's buddy, Al. "We got us a plump visitor."

"Don't kill me," the girl whimpered.

Robin went to her put her arm around the girl's shoulder. "It's all right," she soothed. "We're Americans—we're not going to hurt you. Who are you, and what are you doing wandering around the mountains?"

All the girl could do was sob her name: Jenny Broward. Robin led her to a log and sat her down, waiting until she was composed enough to talk. Several of the mountain men melted back into the forest to keep a lookout. Jeb leaned against a tree and pulled out his chewing tobacco. Chris unsheathed his nine-inch Confederate Bowie and practiced throwing it into a poplar tree.

"Where am I?" Jenny sniffed.

"Georgia, honey. This is the Chattahoochee."

Fresh wails came from the girl, who clung to Robin like a baby. "I'm so far from home, she sobbed.

"Where's home, Jenny?" Robin asked the sweater-clad girl.

"Chattanooga, Tennessee."

Robin and Jeb looked at each other. How in the hell did Jenny get so far away? Robin soothed her and said she and her companions were friends.

Finally Jenny stopped crying long enough to tell her story in jerky snatches of words. She and her family—her parents and two sisters—had tried to escape the chaos that hit Chattanooga after the nuclear strike. They were going to get away east into the mountains. They drove as far as they could, then set out on foot, hiking through the snow.

First her younger sister died from eating poison berries. Then exposure weakened her older sister, who caught pneumonia and died.

Then—the pale, pudgy-faced girl with the long, straight black hair shuddered—she and her parents were attacked by a ragged group of wild men who called themselves the Demonheads. They were raving maniacs, Americans gone beserk. They seized all the Browards' food and supplies and beat up the three of them. They raped Jenny's mother while they forced her and her father to watch; then they shot her father. Finally, they slit her mother's throat and laughed while she died.

"They would have done that to me, too, except they didn't—want me because I was so—so fat," Jenny said, her lips quivering. "They decided it would be more fun to leave me in the wilderness—bear bait, they kept saying."

"You poor child," Robin said, feeling helpless to assuage such horrors.

She'd wandered aimlessly through the forests for an unknown length of time, Jenny said. For the first time in her life, she was glad she was fat—it kept her alive. She stumbled onto an empty log cabin and found meager food supplies. She lived there until the weather warmed and the food ran out, then started wandering again, disoriented.

"I wanted to go home," she said. "And I'm going

the wrong way."

Robin shook her head. "You've found a new home, Jenny." Quickly she told the girl about the invasion of Russians and Cubans and their infiltration into the hills, and about the mountain folk who were resisting. She and the men were on their way now to raid a Russian supply station that had been set up not far away.

"Please let me join you!" the girl begged. Her eyes were filled with desperation. "I want to help!"

Robin looked at Jeb. "Of course she's part of the family now," Jeb said. "But I don't know about the raids. She ain't got no training."

"We can't just leave her here," Robin said.

"Nope. And we can't go back, either, not if we want to hit that supply post while it's most vulnerable." Jeb spat out brown juice.

"Please," begged Jenny, "I'll do whatever you want me to."

Jeb studied her. "You brave, Jenny?"

Her lips tightened and she squared her shoulders. "Yes."

"How's your aim?"

"Well, I won my high school dart championship."

"Then I got me an idea. You eat and drink whatever you want, right quick, then we'll be on our way."

The Russian supply post was set up in an abandoned shingle-board cabin perched on a mountainside, with a sweeping view of blue-green hills and valleys to the south. It was accessed by a dirt road that split off from a two-lane asphalt road that wound through the hills. Bordered by strangely full-blooming azalea and rhododendron bushes, it looked more like a cozy hideaway than a strategic point in a supply line for advancing armies.

The Russians were not advertising their presence. No red hammer-and-sickle flags flew like they did everywhere else the Russians went. This was a covert operation, a supply link for scouting parties and advance troops making their first penetration into the interior of the United States, wiping out resistance as they pushed inland. Besides food, the Russians were stockpiling arms and ammunition, including bazookas. Apparently they were planning some heavy action.

Jeb's three able mountain men had spied on the post long enough to determine regular movements of men and supplies. The raid had been planned for a time when Russian manpower was minimal and the likelihood of unexpected arrivals small.

The raiding party crouched on the slope below the cabin, several hundred yards away. Jeb lowered his binoculars. Robin heard her heart pounding like a drum.

"Two sentries, northeast and southwest corners, walking the perimeter," he said. "I'm told there's never more than two others inside. This should be as easy as cherry pie. Once we take the place, we pack out everything we can." He paused. "Of course, there could be a whole mess of Reds in there . . ."

They all knew the risks, of course—that by striking the post, they would be calling attention to their presence, and that the Russians would make a determined counterattack. But they had decided they had to make a stand.

Robin pointed to the sentry at the southwest corner of the cabin. He was lighting up a cigarette. He sat down on a log. His Kalashnikov was strapped to his shoulder. "That one's for me, Jeb."

"You got him," Jeb said. He gave out instructions. "Caleb, cover Robin here. Al and Hiram, you guys circle around to the northeast side. Chris, you and me's gonna bust in that door as soon as the sentries go down. Everyone to their places." He turned to Jenny. "I got a special job for you, Jenny. Follow me."

Jeb led the fat girl through the brush around to the north side of the cabin, stopping near the edge of the dirt road. "You stay here low and out of sight, and be real quiet. But if you see anything coming down that road, I want you to throw this at them." He pulled a small oval object from a pouch on his hunting vest.

"A grenade!" gasped Jenny.

"That's right. You think you can do it?"

She swallowed and nodded. "What do I do?"

Jeb showed her how to hold the grenade and pull the pin. "Once you pull that pin, you gotta heave that thing away from you and dive into the bushes. Got it?"

Jenny nodded solemnly.

"Good girl. Chances are, you won't have to use it. You're our safety backup, and we're counting on you." Jeb gave her a friendly tap on the shoulder and slid out into the brush.

Robin raised her rifle and sighted on the Russian soldier. She had been forced to kill to save herself, but this seemed so—cold blooded! She was surprised at how calm and detached she felt. This wasn't a person, after all—not another human being in the cross-hairs—he was the *enemy* of all Americans. *Blood for blood.*

On the signal from Jeb, she squeezed the trigger without hesitation. The rifle cracked and she absorbed the kickback. It seemed like forever before the bullet reached its target, tearing through the chest, sending the man flying backward into a twisted, red-splattered heap.

An instant later, Jeb's M16 cut down the second sentry.

Suddenly five Russians stormed out of a nearby concealment, screaming and shouting. Three were partially dressed and looked like they had grabbed their weapons in a hurry. It must be a secret bunker, Robin thought.

The Russians started spraying bullets everywhere. Robin stood stupidly for a moment, unbelieving, and then dove for cover. She crawled on her belly, dragging along her rifle, until she was well into the bushes.

Jeb and the mountain men were shouting and returning the fire. So much dust was kicked up that Robin couldn't see clearly what was going on. She heard screams as men died, but she didn't know if they were American or Russian. She pulled up her rifle and tried to sight into the cloud of dust.

She spotted Jeb crouched behind a tree, his finger down on the trigger of his spitting machine gun. He yelped and fell backward, clutching his right arm at the shoulder. Bullets bit through the dirt around him, and he rolled, trying to avoid getting hit again.

"Jeb!" Robin shrieked. She crouched low and ran toward him, but he waved her back.

"Forget it!" he yelled at her. "I'm okay—it's a flesh wound. Get inside if you can—there's at least one or two holed up in that cabin!"

"But—"

"Shut up and move! We'll handle it here."

There was no time to think about it; Robin picked up her rifle and looked for a clear run at the cabin. She saw Chris on his belly nearby, and managed to get his attention and signal what she was going to do. He nodded that he would follow.

Just as Robin rose to make a dash for it, Jenny appeared out of the dust, running and puffing as fast as she could, a wild look on her pudgy face. She yanked the pin on the grenade and hurled it at the three Russians who were still alive and holding everyone at bay with their spraying bullets.

Robin sprinted for the cabin as the grenade went off, tearing the Russians into pieces. The concussion nearly knocked her off her feet; she stumbled and went on.

With Chris on her heels, she burst through the cabin door. Inside was a Russian who was standing at a window, firing out with a Kalashnikov. Startled, he hesitated for a split second before turning the barrel on Robin. But he never pulled the trigger. Chris's well-thrown Bowie skewered him neatly through the heart.

The supply post was theirs.

As soon as she realized the fight was over, Robin burst into tears. The tears came in a great gush, then were over as suddenly as they had started. She had killed a man without being under attack. But this was war—this is what it was like. She experienced a dizzying surge of triumph. She had killed an enemy, and she knew he would not be the last.

CHAPTER ELEVEN

Dr. Sheila de Camp, head psychologist from White Sands, had a fascination with Col. Dean Sturgis. Fascination tinged with a healthy degree of desire. After all, she was as red-blooded as any young American woman, and wasn't Sturgis a red-blooded American man?

At first, she hadn't liked Sturgis. Loathed him, in fact, for being what she thought was an arrogant male chauvinist—her typically dim view of the opposite sex. Dr. Steely de Camp, they called her behind her back at White Sands. The Ice Queen, unapproachable, unconquerable by mere mortal men; competent, efficient, but somewhat unhuman.

When she met Sturgis, he had acted like he knew best, had *all* the answers, didn't have a thing to learn from any woman. They'd argued heatedly over how to treat psychologically distressed soldiers. She'd had to concede he was right and she was wrong.

In the process, she suddenly discovered how sexy he was. She was mesmerized by his gray bedroom eyes and longed to touch the hard muscles of his broad chest—not to mention unzip his trousers. Sturgis was, she decided, the Ultimate Male. She bet he was a real powerhouse in the sack.

For de Camp, an attractive woman, a long time had passed since her last romantic involvement. In fact, it was so long ago it seemed like it never happened. She had been left with a broken affair and a broken heart, and she'd tried to heal the wounds by throwing herself into her military work. Sturgis was the first man she had met since then who made her want to come out of her cocoon.

So, for the first time in years, de Camp began fretting and fussing over her appearance. In her early thirties, she was still quite attractive, she was happy to note. Her figure was pleasantly full and womanly. She rearranged her dark blond hair to a more flattering style, curly at the ends.

Sturgis's indifference to her only fanned the flames of her desire. She had snuck a peek at his personnel file and gleaned bits of gossip. She was thrilled to find out his wife had filed for a divorce two years ago. So what if he wanted to get back together with her? That woman was thousands of miles away—probably dead. Even if Sturgis had been married, she still would have considered him fair game. All's fair, they say, in love and war. This was definitely war, and as far as de Camp was concerned, she was going to get him.

But before de Camp could make a dent in the colonel's armor, Sturgis and his unit had left White Sands, sending Sheila into a tailspin of despair. Then luck was with her, for when Sturgis called from Florida and asked White Sands to send out a doctor, she knew she was the only C.A.D.S.-trained doc at

White Sands. That meant she would see him again!

She'd been here at the Okefenokee base for days now, and Sturgis was still giving her the cold shoulder. What was he, a priest? Maybe one of those disgusting swampwomen had her hooks into him. De Camp distinctly did not like the tall, leggy one who called herself Dieter. Nor did she like the look in Dieter's eye every time she was around Sturgis.

The jealousy only bolstered her resolve. Underneath her revamped, more feminine appearance, de Camp was tough as nails and had the determination of a hungry hunter. They didn't call her Steely de Camp for nothing.

The next airdrop over the Okefenokee came on a clear, beautiful day. The sky was a crystal blue and the vegetation shimmered a brilliant green, mirrored by the sluggish waters of the swamp. It was the kind of dreamy day that made one forget there ever was such a thing as nuclear war. Even the crocodiles seemed pacified.

White Sands' jerry-rigged prop planes droned over the swamp, releasing their much-needed cargoes in a matter of minutes. Sturgis dispatched a team to round up the bundles of supplies and collect the men who had parachuted down. "We're supposed to get some new recruits," he told Tranh Van Noc inside the command hut. "Make sure they're all accounted for, then bring them to the Rhino for muster."

"Yes, sir, Colonel, I'm on my way."

No sooner than Van Noc had departed than Sheila de Camp poked her head in the door. She was all suited up, for reasons Sturgis couldn't fathom and didn't want to waste time trying to. He scowled and sighed. Every time he turned around, de Camp was there, like a puppy. She seemed to be unable to content herself with running the medical division at White Sands. She had to come here!

The suit looked strange on her, and she stood oddly in it. Maybe it was because she was a woman, and Sturgis's idea of women was that they should never be seven feet tall.

"Reporting for medical duty," she announced.

"The vaccine for the blackwater fever is supposed to be in this drop," Sturgis said. "The men have been instructed to take the packages directly to the infirmary." Since the death of Smythe, the previous medic, two more men had contracted the fever but had survived.

"I know," she said. "But no one knows positively whether or not the vaccine will work. Maybe, like the swine-flu vaccine used decades ago, it will make matters worse. Your men will be inoculated anyway," she finished firmly.

"I'm sure that's fine," he said. "I hope you're ready for my new-recruit's test right after that."

Her scowl darkened. What was he talking about? "What test?" she demanded.

"You know—my proficiency test. If I may remind you, Dr. de Camp, you must have the ability to use the C.A.D.S. suit. You will have a brief check-out, along with the other new arrivals."

Sturgis reached for the pack of cigarettes on his desk and jammed one into his mouth. "Think you can do as well as the men, Sheila?" He smiled. "There will be no allowances for your being a woman."

"I've been practicing," de Camp said. "I'm *good*."

Sturgis was trying to get a match lit. The dampness of the swamp made the matches a little soggy. His butane lighter had long since run out of fuel. "Sure," he said sardonically without looking at her. "When I want a demonstration I'll let you know. Get busy—"

His words were cut off by a sharp whistle of a projectile over his head. He flattened himself on the desk. Behind him, a dart was imbedded halfway in the dirty log of the hut.

He jumped up and stared at it, momentarily stunned. Then he turned in fury on de Camp, who was looking in great puzzlement at the smoking weapons tube on the arm of her suit.

"What the hell do you think you're doing?" he shouted, coming at her. "You nearly took my head off!"

She took an awkward step backward. "I—I thought I had all firing positions on lock."

The C.A.D.S. suit was a complicated piece of equipment, and, in untrained hands, was downright dangerous. The weapons customarily fired on verbal command, but the suit could be programmed to fire by manual control in case verbal commands weren't possible. There also were varying degrees of motion sensitivity that enabled weapons to be fired by movement of the arms alone.

"You *thought*!" Sturgis seized the arm of her suit and punched in a code on the keypad. The stupid woman was a walking arsenal ready to blast at any moment. She could have accidentally shot off anything, including machine-gun fire and E-balls. Lucky for him it hadn't been an E-ball—he'd have been vaporized.

"I'm terribly sorry, Colonel, truly I am," de Camp gushed. "I don't know what to say . . ."

Sturgis was livid. "If we weren't at war and under extraordinary circumstances, I'd have you thrown in the clink and court-martialed for assaulting a superior officer," he said through clenched teeth. "Get out of that suit before you endanger the lives of my men! You will confine yourself to infirmary quarters until I send for you. Do you copy, Doctor?"

She saluted awkwardly and turned to go, nearly tripping over Tranh in the process. Tranh looked at the hole in the wall.

Sturgis stalked back to his desk. He picked what was left of his burning cigarette off the floor, dusted it off, and took a drag. Damn female. He was stuck with her, too. White Sands had sent her—and he couldn't send her back. God, what would he do? What *could* he do?

Tranh saluted smartly. "Colonel, sir, the new recruits are mustered and ready for inspection."

Sturgis put out his cigarette. "I'll be right there. Any—other problems?"

"Nothing major. All personnel and packages have been accounted for against the manifest. Two suits sustained minor damage in the drop, but they should be easy to fix."

Sturgis took the inventory list of the drop from Tranh and quickly looked it over. "Make certain that Dr. de Camp gets her job started right away. Instruct her to have all men vaccinated by sixteen hundred hours. And post a man outside the infirmary with orders not to let de Camp wear her C.A.D.S. suit."

Tranh said, "I understand." He strode away. He had never seen anyone rankle Sturgis so much as Sheila de Camp.

Sturgis went outside, where the newest men stood at attention in two neat rows. They had visors up on their suits. One man smartly saluted. "Sgt. Mark Britten, sir, with replacement troops, reporting for duty."

Sturgis returned the salute, then said, "At ease, men."

He gave a brief speech welcoming the recruits to the C.A.D.S. base, and summarizing the latest engagement at Disney World. "I'm not going to give you a lot of flag-waving bullshit," he told them. "Until White Sands and whatever else is left of the U.S. military get back on their feet, *we're it*. We've been able to give the Reds some good setbacks, but the odds against us are growing every day. We are increasingly outmanned—but not outgunned *or* outsmarted." A murmur of laughter rose from the men.

"Our next objective is to head north to Chesapeake Bay. The Soviets are repairing the tunnel bridge and modifying the highway for a massive deployment of troops south and west. We will attack and destroy their position, taking no prisoners. The Omega Force has distinguished itself for superior fighting performance, and I expect each and every one of you to uphold that reputation. I'm not saying it's going to be easy. It's going to be damn tough. But you wouldn't be here if you weren't capable of doing the job."

Sturgis scanned the solemn faces. "We'll push out as soon as possible, no later han seventy-two hours from now. Some of you will have to assemble your own tribikes from the parts that have been dropped today.

"You'll all receive detailed orders at the appropriate time. If any of you haven't used your suit much recently, identify yourselves to Sgt. Billy Dixon here for brush-up training." He pointed to Dixon, who was standing off to one side.

"In addition, everyone will have his proficiency in the C.A.D.S. suit tested. We've already had a small accident—I don't want to waste much ammo during the test, though. Anybody here feel they need a refresher before you're tested?"

No one spoke up.

"I must warn you," Sturgis added, "it's hell up north. That's all, men. Any questions?"

"Sir, who are all those gorgeous chicks around here?" one man in the second row piped up. Laughter broke out, along with yelps of "Yeah!" "Wahoo!" and a few wolf whistles and scattered applause.

Sturgis grinned. "I'm glad to see there's nothing wrong with anyone's eyesight. The *ladies*—" he emphasized the word—"you see are liberated prisoners of war. Formerly they were wives and girlfriends in respectable Southern communities. When we set up base here, we found them held captive by a tribe of swamp marauders. The Swampers are gone and the women now live freely in the swamp. Their village isn't far away. They come around to help us out—you might say we're in a mutual-assist mode."

"Does anything go, Colonel?" the same man asked, winking.

"What you do on your own time is your own

business," Sturgis answered crisply. "But I expect you to behave like gentlemen. They're our *allies*, and I intend to keep it that way. Anything else?"

"Sir," Britten said, "why is everything so green here? I know it's April, but everywhere else, it's still bare."

"This is a low-rad area," Sturgis explained. "My best guess is that there's a curtain of moisture that has warmed and protected the swamp, due to a weather alteration."

"Well, it's a welcome sight to all of us, Colonel—that plus the ladies. Everything else around the country is damned depressing."

Another new recruit spoke up. "Does low-rad mean the fresh food around here is safe to eat?"

"Up to a point," Sturgis said. "We've found the fish and fowl safe. Fruits are turning, however. We've noticed the new fruit, the first to ripen since the nukes, is often rotten on the inside. Some of it also has an ashen texture—it looks fine until you touch it, and then it crumbles. I advise you not to eat any fruit that has not been inspected here at the base first."

Sturgis clasped his hands behind his back. "Nothing else? Dixon will give you your billets. Dismissed. Sergeant Britten, one moment, please." He waved the man over to him. "Britten," he said in a low voice, "tell me what's really going on at White Sands." He stared the crew-cut youth directly in the eye.

"I don't quite know what you mean, sir."

"I think you *do*." Sturgis clapped him on the shoulder. "Loosen up, man, it's all right. We're not so formal most of the time." The two of them started walking to the command center, where he told Britten to unsuit. He went around behind his desk and took two cans from a bottom drawer. "Have a seat, Britten, and a drink."

"Beer!" exclaimed the new sergeant.

"Rad-free. Been saving it for an occasion. This seems like one." Sturgis shoved a can across the desk to Britten. They popped the tops and took big gulps.

"I never thought I'd taste beer again," Britten said, wiping the back of his hand across his mouth.

"Even warm, it still tastes damn good," Sturgis said. He exhaled lazily and propped his feet up on his desk. He watched Britten slump a little as he relaxed. Britten was a handsome youth in his mid-twenties, with dark, short-cropped hair and deep brown eyes that women probably went for. Sturgis had a keen intuition for spotting good men, and Britten definitely had that look.

"As I was asking . . ." Sturgis prompted.

"Yes, about White Sands," Britten looked around nervously. "You want my honest opinion?"

"I'm not asking for bullshit, Sergeant."

"My feeling is, the whole place is going out of control."

Sturgis wasn't surprised. He'd sensed a creeping chaos in his last few satellite talks with Headquarters. He took a big draught of beer.

"It's the refugees, sir," Britten went on. "They're pouring in from everywhere, thousands of them. The place is jammed to the gills. We're not turning anyone away. We've got people in various stages of radiation sickness, and a whole pack of thieves. The stealing and violence is getting out of hand."

"What's President Williamson doing about it?"

"As much as he can, sir. The jail and the sick bay are full to overflowing."

Sturgis nodded, more to himself than to Britten. The situation at White Sands undoubtedly would get worse. He would have to rely less and less on Headquarters for direction and assistance. As long as some military hotshot like that Colonel Clearwell didn't get the idea for another coup, Williamson ought to be able to cope. Sturgis remembered Clearwell's attempted takeover, and how he'd ousted him. He was too far away to help White Sands now, and besides that, he had his own job to do.

Sturgis changed the subject. "I see from the manifest that you have an outstanding rating in suit work, Mark."

"Thank you, sir."

Sturgis pulled out his pack of cigarettes and offered one to Britten, who accepted. "I have a job for you," Sturgis said. "Our doc, who just arrived in the airdrop before, is pretty green with the suit. We've got to take de Camp with us when we leave, so I want you to do some crash training."

"Of course, Colonel. No problem. I'll get him shaped up in nothing flat."

"*Her*, Britten. The doc is a she." Sturgis was amused at the startled look on Britten's face. "You have my permission to do whatever is necessary to get her combat ready." He crooked a wicked smile. "She can be difficult."

"What's the matter, Doc—can't find the vein?" Sturgis inhaled on his cigarette while Dr. de Camp poked his bare forearm. He was sitting at a table inside the sick bay with his arm laid out, palm side up, like a sacrificial offering. He was the first in the C.A.D.S. camp to get the swamp-fever vaccine. The hypodermic rested on the table beside him while de Camp took an extraordinarily long time to probe for the ideal spot near the indent of his elbow. The blue rope of his vein stood out plainly from his muscled flesh.

"Your sleeve isn't rolled up high enough," de Camp said, her cheeks reddening. She gave the sleeve a couple more turns up his bicep and retied the slim rubber hose that served as a tourniquet. The vein in his forearm bulged a bit. "That's better," she said pressing the vein with her thumb. "Would you please put that cigarette out, Colonel?"

He took a last drag and dropped the cigarette to the floor, where he crushed it with his booted heel.

"There has to be *some* observance of health rules in this place," de Camp said frostily. "Cigarettes are unhealthy."

"So's World War Three, Doc," Sturgis said. "I got more than fifty men out there waiting their turn, so hurry up."

She then deftly slid the needle into his vein and injected the vaccine. She removed the tourniquet and took a piece of cotton dipped in alcohol and dabbed at the spot of blood that rose at the prick. Then she put a piece of adhesive over the cotton. "There."

Sturgis unrolled his sleeve and stood up.

"Just a moment, Colonel," de Camp said. "There's something I want to discuss with you." She fiddled with her instruments as she talked. "I want a facial skin patch from you, and also from every one of your men, to determine radiation exposure."

Sturgis grunted.

"There are some odd dots on your face," she went on. She looked up at him. "I'd like to skin-patch you now."

Sturgis felt a pang in his stomach as his muscles tightened. "Dots? What are you talking about?" he said gruffly.

"You've had your helmet open too much in high-rad areas. I think I know why." She pointed to the flattened cigarette butt on the floor. "You're opening your helmet to smoke, aren't you?"

Sturgis narrowed his smoky gray eyes at de Camp. "I don't need an antismoking lecture, Corporal. Just tell me the bottom line."

Her face creased in exasperation and she pushed her blond hair back from her face. "The bottom line, Colonel, is you're violating regulations. We need you, and you're pushing it. If you want to stick around, you have to quit smoking. Otherwise, Lieutenant Van Noc is going to find himself succeeding you in command very quickly." She stuck a sticky patch on his face and ripped it off quickly. "There, it's done."

Sturgis strode outside. He resented her clucking at him about his smoking, but he was even angrier that she was right. She had hit him with a real zinger. Not that he was afraid to die—he'd gotten over that fear months ago. It was the idea of dying foolishly. If he had to die, it would be by an enemy bullet, not because he smoked.

He rubbed the raw spot on his cheek. "Shit," he said, and walked on.

Hours later, long after the camp had quieted down for the night, Sturgis lay on his makeshift bed on the floor of his hut, trying to numb his mind beyond thought. Dixon, Van Noc, and some of the other men had disappeared early for a night of diversion with the swamp girls. He didn't stop them.

He was alone. Despite de Camp's warning, he was not ready to kick the nicotine habit, and ghostly wisps of smoke from his burning cigarette curled and drifted toward the vent hole in the roof.

A full moon lit up the night outside, so that he could see shadowy silhouettes of the objects in his hut. The embers of his cigarette glowed orange-red. The night was cool, but warm enough for him to be naked beneath his standard-issue blanket.

He was trying not to think of anything, especially Robin, but was having little success. He missed her terribly, wanted her badly. So many obstacles stood in the way. Time and time again, he had fantasized about turning his back on the whole nuke mess the country was in, finding Robin and somehow getting her to some forgotten corner of the world. But duty was duty, and there probably wasn't any such place, anyway.

A cloud passed over the moon and the night around him turned inky. He felt for the empty C-ration can that was his ashtray and dropped the butt in, hearing it hiss out in the water in the bottom. He knew that sleep would not come for a long time, if at all, and was just about to get up when the door opened quietly and then closed. Someone was inside, but in the pitch-blackness, Sturgis could see nothing.

He reached out beside the straw mattress and

grasped his 9mm Beretta Parabellum semiautomatic. Had someone slipped past the sentries?

"Who's there?" he said, cocking the firing pin. No answer came, and he strained for sounds.

As suddenly as it had disappeared, the moon slipped from behind the clouds. A face materialized in the darkness, so close to Sturgis that he could smell the perfume. He recognized the face in the same instant.

"Dieter! What are you doing, sneaking in here like that? You could have gotten yourself shot!" He locked the firing pin.

She bent down and took the gun carefully from his hand. Her touch was satiny and her skin was full of sweet tropical fragrance. She was naked, having dropped her clothing by the door, and the whiteness of her lush, rounded contours shone in the moonlight.

"I had this feeling I ought to be here tonight," she said.

He made room for her and she slipped beneath the cover, folding herself into his welcoming embrace. She was hot, on fire, and her heat spread through him like spontaneous combustion. It was just the kind of exquisite oblivion he needed.

CHAPTER TWELVE

"Impossible!" shrieked Supreme Marshal Mikhail Veloshnikov. He slammed his big fist down onto his desk so hard that everything on it—coffee cup, pens, paperweight, and wire baskets full of papers—jumped and rattled.

The cipher clerk, Vasily Dubronin, couldn't tell from the fury written all over the supreme marshal's face whether or not he would shoot Dubronin simply for bringing bad news. Stranger things had happened lately in the American Occupied War Zone. Dubronin eyed the Turganev service revolver which gleamed in Veloshnikov's hip holster. He backed away but couldn't go too far—the office inside the giant nuclear attack sub *Lenin* was full of furniture.

"I'm afraid it's true about Disney World, Supreme Marshal," the clerk said in a small voice. "I'm sorry . . ."

"It can't be—it's a false report," screamed Veloshnikov. *"Nyet!"*

"Unfortunately not, sir."

"You stupid idiot! It's *disinformation*. The Americans could not possibly have destroyed the Cuban base in Florida."

Dubronin shrugged helplessly. "The communiqué was confirmed, verified, and validated."

Veloshnikov opened his other clenched fist and smoothed the wad of paper crumpled inside. He reread the decoded message, which reported that a detachment of the American Blacksuits—the equivalent of the Russian Spetsnaz-11 Graysuits—had raided and demolished the Cuban foothold, leaving no survivors.

Furthermore, the message went on—and this was what had made the legendary Veloshnikov temper explode—the commandos also had destroyed a squad of Russian White Wolfs. Cubans were expendable, and if they wanted to humiliate themselves by their stupidity and cowardice, that was no skin off his teeth. But Russians were a different matter. Russians in a squad of White Wolfs should have been able to mop up ground forces, even Blacksuits, in nothing flat.

He gritted his teeth. How would the Americans say it? *"Shit,"* he hissed.

He looked up at Dubronin, who had managed to inch his way over to the hatch. "Will there be anything else, Supreme Marshal?"

"Get out of my sight!"

The cipher clerk was only too glad to obey.

Still cursing beneath his breath, Veloshnikov stuffed the communiqué in his uniform pocket and stormed out of the tiny office, ducking and squeezing through the passageway. Despite the *Lenin*'s huge size—nearly three hundred meters—much of its interior was cramped and confined, since the bulk of its space was taken up by its reactors and enormous store of nuclear warheads. Ample space also was given over to the numerous, sophisticated command centers and war-theater rooms, and to Velochnikov's private quarters. Beyond that, offices and crew quarters were mere niches.

Veloshnikov pushed through the sub like a steam locomotive, flattening crew members in his way against the gray bulkheads. They saluted him sharply.

When he reached the giant War Command Center, he threw out a couple of lieutenants who were poring over maps and pulled the hatch door closed. Then he got on the ship's intercom and paged Capt. Ilya Guriev, bellowing at him to report to War Center A immediately.

That done, Veloshnikov prepared to go to work. He yanked at the buttons of his jacket, pulled it off and threw it on a chair. He rolled his shirtsleeves up to the elbows.

The War Command Center was shaped like the inside of a ball. The skin of the ball provided 360 degrees of backlit screens that displayed dozens of combinations of maps, grids, and charts of all military operations in all theaters.

The wall illustrations were controlled by a powerful, fast computer. The fact that it was Japanese-designed and far superior to the bulky, slow Russians computers, which were constantly breaking down, did not bother Veloshnikov's Russian pride in the least. The Soviets had won the technological secrets fair and square by blackmailing a hapless Japanese electronics executive who had a weakness for Russian prostitutes whenever he traveled to Moscow. The prostitutes, of course, just happened to be working for the KGB.

All military movements were reported to various command centers, which the *Lenin* was one. The computers—smaller and less sophisticated ones in all the centers worldwide—provided ground, air, and naval officers with constantly updated information. Officers also were able to do strategic planning with endless scenarios, all plotted and spit out quickly by computer. Data could be instantly projected onto screens and blank walls.

The computer equipment—a compact central processor with tape drives, several terminals, and dot-matrix printers—was complemented by a bank of communications equipment, the world's best. Various colored lights blinked on and off. Along part of the curvature in the wall, a row of telexes were in perpetual motion, printing out coded messages going back and forth between military units and between the *Lenin* and the Kremlin in Moscow.

Veloshnikov entered his password on the computer keyboard and logged on to the system. His password was BUDDYBOY. He had used it for decades, ever since he served as a military attache to the North Vietnamese during the Vietnam War. Out on a rutted, muddy road near Da Nang one wet day, he and his driver stopped to fix a flat and were ambushed by a half-crazed American G.I. waving a machine gun at them. The man was deep in enemy territory, perhaps hopped up on drugs—or insanely brave.

The G.I. staggered up to Veloshnikov, jammed the

M16 into his rubs, and slurred, "Yer time's up, buddy boy." Veloshnikov pretended to stumble backward, and in so doing, shot his foot out and tripped the American, who was weak and unsteady on his feet. Before the G.I. knew what was happening, he was sprawled on his back with Veloshnikov's knife plunged into his neck up to the hilt—and he was very dead.

Veloshnikov took the M16 as a trophy. He often thought of the G.I. who had called him buddy boy. A knife in the jugular was just what he had done now to America itself.

When Guriev arrived, breathless from having jog-trotted the nearly entire length of the 220-meter sub plus two levels down, Veloshnikov handed him the communiqué without preamble.

Guriev whistled. "Fuck your mother!"

"Damn right, 'fuck your mother.' "

"What does Moscow say about it?"

"Moscow doesn't know yet. The Havana message is for my eyes only." Veloshnikov opened a humidor and took out one of his favorite Cuban cigars. He rolled it around his lips and then bit off the end and spat it out.

Guriev handed the crumpled paper back to him. "A report must be made, Supreme Marshal."

Veloshnikov nodded impatiently as he lit his cigar. That was Guriev's biggest shortcoming. He was a damn fine officer, but was obstinate and stodgy when it came to following rules. Everything had to be by the book. Would he never learn that anything of importance was *never* done by the book?

"Yes, yes," Veloshnikov said, "a report will be

made—in due time. You have an astonishingly short memory, Ilya Ivanovitch. Have you forgotten the recent reprimand?" The supreme marshal himself was still smarting over that one—the stinging rebuke from the Premier concerning the destruction the Blacksuits had done in Charleston not long ago. Veloshnikov was personally upbraided by the commander in chief of the Soviet armed forces for not thwarting the attack. The Premier had no appreciation for the fact that the *Lenin* herself had barely escaped injury in the nick of time—due to Veloshnikov's brilliance.

Veloshnikov snorted. What did those potatoheads in the Kremlin know, anyway? They weren't at the front. Still, he could not afford many more official reprimands without damaging his career and his rank.

Guriev looked uncomfortable at the reminder. He was an ambitious man, Veloshnikov knew, and reprimands in the dossier carried a powerful sting.

"I will file a full report," Veloshnikov assured him, "*after* we engage the Blacksuits in a retaliatory strike and destroy them."

Guriev grinned as he suddenly realized what the supreme marshal was proposing. The damage in Florida would be minimized by the glory of victory. If the *Lenin* had a role, commendations and medals would be in the offing for him.

"What can I do, Supreme Marshal?" Guriev asked eagerly.

Veloshnikov worked the keyboard of his computer terminal. "First, there is a small matter of a cipher clerk. Dubronin."

"Of course. I noticed he seemed sick today—I'll

have him quarantined right away." The captain picked up a telephone receiver. "Will measles do?"

"Yes." Veloshnikov smiled. Cipher clerks were under strict orders not to discuss communiqués with anyone, but he was taking no chances. "Look here," he said as Guriev got off the phone. He manipulated the keyboard.

Around them, in 360 degrees, a new set of gridded maps sprang into focus. The maps were speckled with colored dots to show troop positions. Veloshnikov focused in on the Eastern seaboard of the United States and magnified it before them.

"The communiqué says nothing about lost documents, Captain." He highlighted the Chesapeake Bay area in blue. "We must assume, however, that our Cuban comrades were not able to destroy all records at the base, and that the American imperialists have discovered our Chesapeake Bay plan."

Veloshnikov put a black dot at Orlando for the Disney World disaster. "We must also assume that the Americans will head straight for Chesapeake. Do you agree, Captain?"

Guriev nodded vigorously.

"Good." Veloshnikov chomped down on his cigar. "Now, allowing for time to treat the wounded, repair machinery, et cetera, plus estimated ground travel speeds . . ." his voice trailed off as he punched in factors. The computer responded by highlighting the Georgia coast in yellow.

Veloshnikov stood and ran his finger up and down the highlighted area. "The Omega Force is most likely within this sector," he announced. "Anywhere from the Okefenokee up to Savannah. And we are here."

He tapped the keys, and a red dot appeared in the Atlantic Ocean just south of Washington, D.C.

The supreme marshal poked Guriev's chest. "If you were in command, Captain, what would you do?"

Guriev cleared his throat and straightened himself. He was not often asked his opinion. He pretended to study the map while he composed his thoughts.

"I would send ground and air troops south," he said at length, "to hit them in Georgia. As backup I would deploy troops north to Chesapeake, and establish a defense line well to the south and west of the tunnel—here." He pointed to the map. "I would position the Graysuits close on red alert. Finally, I would increase air reconnaissance along the Georgia coast, penetrating inland to Macon and Atlanta, in case the imperialists choose to travel by an interior route."

Veloshnikov nodded slowly. He would have to watch Guriev more closely. He could be a brilliant ally or a formidable opponent, depending on his politics.

"Very good, Captain. My thoughts exactly. Now, if you would please raise General Petrin for me on the teleconference line."

"Take that, you miserable dog! I'll whip you till you beg for mercy!" General Petrin suited action to his words. He sighted his targets and fired, blasting three of them into infinity. *Blam—blam—blam! Boom—boom—boom!* Petrin grinned. These American video games were great fun.

Colonel Boris Kurchiev screamed, "Die! Die!" He

grabbed his joystick and returned fire of his own. Two of his shots went wild but the third blew up its target. "I'm not done yet," he bellowed. "The space attackers must die!"

"We'll see about that!" rejoined Petrin. He was determined to win this round of Space Zap with a complete rout of Kurchiev's spaceship blips. He'd been practicing for days, and now maneuvered his own fleet on the table-screen in deft swoops and dives. "Ay!" he shouted as the last of Kurchiev's ships went up in an electronic explosion.

"Another round!" insisted Kurchiev. "I must have the chance to redeem myself."

But Petrin was tired of Space Zap. "Let's play something else," he said, standing up from the video table. He looked around at the other game machines. These American imperialists certainly indulged themselves in a lot of gadgets, he thought.

The video game room was a lucky find. It was part of the Georgetown mansion on the outskirts of Washington, D.C., which Petrin had selected as the command center for the Graysuits. The mansion and all its furnishings were found intact, and the Soviet officers had wasted no time in installing themselves in the suites.

Petrin, naturally, had taken the largest and most elegant room, and his aide and friend, Kurchiev, hadn't done badly. The mansion offered many diversions and amusements when the officers were off duty: a home fitness center filled with exercise equipment Petrin had never imagined existed; an oak-paneled video game room packed with machines; an entertainment room with a giant television screen, video recorder, and hundreds of movie tapes (mostly depraved American violence and lust, but nevertheless immensely enjoyable); and an incredible stock of wines and liquors, none of which were damaged by radiation.

Petrin picked up his crystal tumbler full of single-malt Scotch and wandered around the room, trying to decide what to play next. He was not wasting time, he told himself; these games required fast reflexes and a high degree of skill. He was preparing for action, merely in a pleasant way.

Kurchiev went to the polished oak bar along one side of the room to seek a refill for his big glass.

"How about Pac-Man?" Kurchiev said. "We haven't played that in a while."

Petrin grunted. "I don't like Pac-Man. It's just a cookie running around eating up dots and ghosts." His glass full, he joined Kurchiev.

Boris pointed to another machine and tried to make out the name. "Don-kee Kong. We haven't played this yet at all. What does 'Donkey Kong' mean?"

Petrin shrugged. "Who knows? Americans are very odd people, clever and brave. They have an obsession with absolute individual freedom. Perhaps this game is better understood by an American." He pushed the button to start the game. It didn't work at first, but, after considerable thumping on Petrin's part, finally came to life with a chirping little tune, then a picture of a zigzag staircase and a big gorilla on top jumping up and down on it.

Petrin and Kurchiev exchanged puzzled glances. They grew even more puzzled when they realized that the game was trying to get a little man up the staircase while the gorilla rolled barrels down at him.

"It must be a gorilla hunt," Kurchiev said. "Except I don't understand why the gorilla is at the top of a staircase instead of in the jungle, and why the hunter is dressed like a worker. Why barrels, and where's the hunter's gun?"

"Forget it," said Petrin, and they moved on to the next machine. "I told you that Americans are inventive geniuses. Perhaps one must need a capitalist mind to create such puzzles."

Petrin was just flopping down in a leather chair when they were interrupted.

"Supreme Marshal Veloshnikov demands your immediate presence at a teleconference, General," said a messenger who stood stiffly at attention in the doorway.

Petrin scowled. Whatever the supreme marshal wanted undoubtedly meant trouble for him. He shot a glance at Kurchiev and handed him his glass of Scotch. "Carry on, friend."

In the media room, the telecommunications linkup was already made. Petrin waited at attention for the image of Veloshnikov to appear on the blank screen. His mind raced to think of reasons for the contact. A teleconference was unusual. He'd already been reprimanded for the Charleston debacle, but he couldn't think of a mistake since then. He hoped his commander wasn't transferring him to another front; Georgetown would be difficult to leave.

When Veloshnikov's stormy face and medal-draped uniform filled the screen, Petrin knew immediately the news was not good. His heart sank.

The supreme marshal allowed his general to stand at ease. He delivered a summary report on Disney World. Petrin blanched and his stomach went hollow.

"We were not aware of the attack," he said. "Rest assured my Graysuits are always ready to deploy, and we received no orders to do so." Petrin was *not* taking the rap for the Cubans *or* for the White Wolfs.

Veloshnikov looked pained. "It is not your fault. I know that. I'll deal with Florida later. What concerns me at the moment is defense of Chesapeake. We must assume the Americans know about it and will attempt to stop us. You must deploy your Spetsnaz-11 troops immediately. Furthermore, you will command them yourself."

"Yes, Supreme Marshal," Petrin said with as much enthusiasm as he could muster at the necessity of leaving the American capital. Perhaps, he consoled himself, the Blacksuits would not attack Chesapeake. He listened raptly as Veloshnikov outlined the action plan. It sounded good throughout.

"The bulk of my Greysuit Commandos should be concentrated around Chesapeake," Petrin agreed. "I can deploy about one hundred and ninety men. All will wear the newer version of the Spetsnaz-11 mechanical suits, with heavy weaponry."

The discussion with Veloshnikov went on for another half-hour. By the time he left the media room, Petrin had gotten over having to leave the comforts of Georgetown. He was not anxious for another fight with the Blacksuits, but this time he might—just might—be able to wrest a victory. The Yankees had surprised him before, but their luck had to run out someday.

He'd set a trap. Knock down the Blacksuit gorillas with a barrel. He smiled. Sure. Easy.

But Petrin knew that the U.S. Blacksuit squad had an exceptional leader—a true warrior, brave and cunning. The trap at Chesapeake would have to be well laid. This was no game!

CHAPTER THIRTEEN

"Okay, men, here's the plan." Sturgis spread out an assortment of maps and papers full of drawings on the table before him. Standing behind him were his most trusted officers: Van Noc, Dixon, Rossiter, Fuentes and MacLeish.

Sturgis also had included Sgt. Mark Britten in the strategy briefing. More and more, he liked Britten's can-do attitude. Plus, the young man had put the new C.A.D.S. men and de Camp through their paces better than he could have. They all passed muster now.

"As we know, the Soviets are rebuilding the Chesapeake Bay Bridge Tunnel in order to facilitate troop movements." Sturgis pointed to the red line on an Exxon map that extended from Norfolk, Virginia, across Chesapeake Bay to the opposite shore. "Our orders are to knock out the bridge beyond any repair, delaying the Soviets and forcing them to find an alternative plan. We're to destroy as many troops and artillery as possible.

"Norfolk, Baltimore and Washington are all Red-occupied zones with plenty of ground, sea, and air forces. Maybe Richmond's occupied by now, too. There is only one feasible approach—from the south." Sturgis took a red pen and drew arrows to the target area.

"But it has a serious disadvantage, in that it takes us into the heavily Red-saturated Norfolk area, and if they encircle us from behind, we're looking at nothing but a vast expanse of water—and one bridge that could be cut off.

"But we have no choice." He put his thumb on the Georgia-Florida border. "From our position here, we've got about seven hundred miles to cover if we take the most direct route up the coast.

"I've decided against that. The Soviets may know we're coming, and the coastal route is going to be under heavy air surveillance. According to the Revengers, we can make our way up inland on a series of secondary highways and roads that are clear of debris and can afford good cover. Depending on the route, these winding roads could double our mileage, but I believe the added safety factor is well worth it."

The men around the table murmured their agreement.

"I don't believe the extra time involved will matter much," Sturgis said. "The Russians probably have already geared up for our attack. In fact, a delay on our part could work to our advantage, since they might begin relaxing their guard."

"What about sending a decoy unit up the coast?" suggested Billy Dixon.

"If I had more men, I would," Sturgis replied. "I

don't have enough to risk. It would have to be a platoon or larger—a squad won't fool the Russians for a minute."

The colonel shuffled through his stack and then handed papers to Dixon and Fuentes. "To minimize enemy detection en route, I'm splitting the force into squads, one for each of you, plus myself. These are the lists of the men under your command, and the routes we'll take. We'll stagger our travel by time, but stick close enough together for defensive response. The rendezvous points are shown on the maps attached." He handed papers to MacLeish and Rossiter. "Fenton and Mickey, here are the orders for the Rhino. You'll have an attachment of eight men on tribikes."

"What are the stats on the bridge itself, Colonel?" asked Van Noc.

"It's actually a complex of connecting tunnels, bridges, and causeways," Sturgis answered. "The whole Chesapeake Bay causeway measures about twenty-three miles in length. Two main tunnels, Thimble Shoal and Chesapeake Channel, run underwater across the bay, about a mile in length each. We won't know the exact situation until we get there, since our maps might be inadequate. The Reds have been changing the facility."

Sturgis looked around the table. "Okay. We'll push out before dawn at oh four hundred hours, heading inland toward Macon, then skirting east. We'll avoid population centers—I don't want to waste time and firepower fighting scavengers if I can help it." He gathered the papers together. "Does anyone have any problems to report?"

The group was silent.

"No reactions to the swamp-fever vaccine?" Silence again. Sturgis was relieved. He didn't need any more complications.

In the eerie hush of predawn, the C.A.D.S. Force pulled out of the Okefenokee on their tribikes, leaving the base in the care of Dieter and her swamp-women. They cleared the swamp easily on their tribikes and struck out through the countryside, following Highway 441 north. They scanned ahead by bouncing radar off various layers in the atmosphere. Sunrise came as they traveled into southern Georgia, but the sun itself was obscured by a lid of gray clouds. More and more, Sturgis had noticed, the sky and earth were taking on a grayish tint.

"Pretty grim, isn't it, Sturge?" Roberto Fuentes' voice crackled in the colonel's headset. Fuentes' squad rode in the lead, just ahead of Sturgis and his unit. "The vegetation looks like it came out and is dying again."

"It is," answered Sturgis. Georgia had always been a lush state, but the vegetation around them was in mixed stages of life and death. Some appeared vibrant and green, while other trees and bushes looked brown and brittle. "It's a whole new world now," he added. "Let's hope the old one comes back."

Sturgis wondered if the entire nation was in a nuclear death throe. Perhaps remote, isolated parts of the Northwest and Canada were still untouched, but sooner or later the drifting nuclear clouds would taint those places, too.

What about the rest of the world? Were the Soviets the new masters of the planet? America was largely cut off from communications with other nations. The absence of news from America's allies led Sturgis to conclude that the Russians hadn't limited their nuclear strike to the U.S.

President Williamson had told him, over the last satellite transmission they'd had before Omega Force left for Chesapeake, that White Sands had gotten word about a so-called Pacific Nuclear Free Zone. Apparently Australia, New Zealand, and the scattered nations in Micronesia agreed not to aid America if the Russians promised not to bomb or occupy their lands.

Sure, thought Sturgis, a Red promise was as good as Hitler's. The Russians would move in when they were ready. So the Aussies were trying to save their own hides! But why not, thought Sturgis; who could blame them? They were on the other side of the globe. And for the time being, at least, it *was* comforting to know that there were some places on earth that radiation and bombs had not destroyed.

"Sturge, we should be coming up on a small population center, but I'm not picking it up on radar," Fenton announced. "Sycamore Grove, original population eight thousand. The highway cuts right through the center of town."

"No sign of *anything*?" asked Sturgis.

"Nothing is registering on my readings—no movements, no buildings. The vector coordinates show we're forty miles from where Sycamore Grove ought to be and heading straight for it, but the sensors say nothing's there."

"Keep monitoring. Advise me if you pick up anything, even the smallest reading."

"Colonel? Private Hawkins here." A new voice with a Southern drawl cut in over the radio.

"Yes, Hawkins?" Sturgis answered. He didn't stand on too many military formalities. Any of his men could address him directly. Nick Hawkins, he knew, was one of the new suitmen airdropped from White Sands, and was riding in Britten's squad behind Sturgis.

"Request permission to advance to the front, sir. Sycamore Grove is—" the voice faltered—"is my hometown."

"Permission granted. Units ahead of Squad Three, make way." Poor devil, thought Sturgis. If the sensors weren't picking up anything, it probably was because there was nothing left of Sycamore Grove, not even matchsticks.

Why would a sleepy Southern town, population eight thousand, be obliterated? Sturgis had lost count of the thousands of towns and villages they'd passed through that were abandoned but still standing. The town couldn't have been hit by a stray Russian missile, or else they'd be picking up intense radiation. The radiation level was virtually nil. But there was an odor now. A bad odor.

Shortly Hawkins zoomed by, bent over his tribike. Sturgis wished there was something he could say to prepare the young man for the shock he was certain was coming, but nothing came to mind that didn't sound like a B-movie.

In a few moments, MacLeish addressed Sturgis over a private channel. "Hawkins wants to go on into town by himself, ahead of everyone else. Under the circumstances, I don't think it's advisable."

"Negative," said Sturgis. "He can go. There's no point in prolonging the agony for him. At least he'll have a few minutes to recover before the rest of us get there. Still no readings?"

"Not a blessed thing."

"I'm coming forward." Sturgis revved up his tribike and maneuvered up along the Rhino.

The first sign the Omega Force had that Hawkins had discovered the fate of Sycamore Grove was a chilling scream. It sounded like a man being tortured—like someone who'd just had his hand severed and was staring at the bloody stump.

Sturgis reacted immediately by shutting down the open radio channel, cutting off another scream. He opened radio links to the squad leaders. "All units, halt!" He came up along Fuentes, who nodded. They accelerated and shot forward.

Sturgis opened a private channel between himself, Fuentes, and Hawkins. "Hawkins! Hawkins! What's happened? Can you hear me?"

The only response he got was the sound of Hawkins throwing up, then choking on his vomit.

"Jesus Christ." Sturgis accelerated again and pulled away from Fuentes. In minutes he made the turn and had reached the outskirts of what once was Sycamore Grove. Stretched in front of him on the Georgian plain were blocks and blocks of flattened, charred rubble—the entire town had been burned to the ground. Sturgis saw no blast scars, so the place hadn't been bombed.

"Hawkins, where are you?" The choking sounds

from the private were replaced by a moaning and whimpering. "Hawkins?"

Sturgis commanded his sensors "Mode red," and located his man further into the center of the ruins. Fuentes screeched to a stop beside him. They got off their bikes and went on foot, bounding in long, high strides in the C.A.D.S. suits. Everywhere around them were black chunks and pieces. Nothing moved; the only sounds came over the radio from Hawkins.

Sturgis and Fuentes found Hawkins in the town cemetery. The entire place was filled with unburied bodies. Men, women, and children, fallen in concentric circles around a Civil War monument in the cemetery's center. They all appeared arranged in family groups. In their best clothes. Many showed signs of rad poisoning—bald heads even on children, red pockmarks on their decaying faces. Hawkins was in the middle of the field, clawing through the piles of putrefying globs of flesh.

With his hydraulic strength, he was tossing bodies and parts of bodies as if they were made of papier mache. "Mother! Dad! Tommy!" he screamed over and over again.

The scenario of what had happened in Sycamore Grove hit Sturgis in a staggering flash: a small town in the backroads of America hears about the nuclear disaster, the destruction of its major cities, the bringing of the nation to her knees. The townspeople, suddenly cut off from supplies and communications, realize they face one of two fates—slow death by starvation or radiation, or torture and subjugation by the Russians, who would inevitably arrive. So they take their fate into their own hands, and burn their homes and town to the ground, then come here and commit collective suicide. Another Jonestown. Only—

Sturgis felt his own stomach rebelling, and swallowed down the nausea. It was one of the most horrible spectacles he had seen yet. "Hawkins!" he shouted. "Get out of there immediately!"

Private Hawkins ignored him.

"Hawkins! Get out, on the double!"

Hawkins paused long enough to look up and glare at Sturgis and Fuentes. His eyes were wild, like those of a mad dog. "Leave me alone, Colonel. Go away." He went back to pawing through the remains.

Sturgis didn't know how the private could stand it. Judging from the state of decay, the bodies had been there quite a while. The stench—if the suit didn't protect him—would be unbearable, Sturgis was sure. But Hawkins was oblivious to any health danger.

"Nick," Sturgis said in a gentler voice, "there's nothing there for you. You won't recognize anyone. Let's go."

"I will *too* recognize them! I've got to find them!" Hawkins started to sob. "Why did you do this to them, God? *Why did you do this?*"

Fuentes addressed Sturgis on a private channel. "He's dangerous in that suit, Colonel. He could go berserk and fire on you."

"He's alrady flipped. We'll have to grab him. Let's split up." Sturgis and Fuentes began moving in opposite directions to come at Hawkins from different sides.

Hawkins screamed. He tore off his helmet and threw it with vehemence into the decaying mass.

"Don't come near me!" he shouted at Sturgis and Fuentes. "Why can't you just *leave me alone*?"

"We need you to rejoin the men," Sturgis said calmly. "Everyone is waiting for you."

"Back off!" Hawkins raised his arm and loosed a stream of machine-gun fire at Sturgis. The bullets bounced off the colonel's suit and ricocheted, thumping into the bodies on the ground. "That's just a warning, sir. I want to stay here."

For a moment, Hawkins stood and stared at Sturgis. Then he said, "God, sir, I'm sorry." He pointed his finger at his face and fired an E-ball. Blood, brain matter, and bits of skull splattered Sturgis and Fuentes. Hawkins's headless suit swayed and then tumbled into the mass grave.

Well into the next day, Sturgis still couldn't shake the grisly image from his mind: Nick Hawkins standing on the decaying remains of his family and friends, joining them in their mass suicidal grave. The tragedy had cast a somber mood over the entire Omega Force. While Sturgis knew he could not afford to have men who would crack under pressure—and therefore Hawkins's death was a cruel blessing of sorts—it still put a knot in his throat.

At 1200 hours they encountered a group of Revengers, heading south to join up with another unit of American irregulars. They knew of the C.A.D.S. unit, so there was no problem. Sturgis asked them about Robin.

"That's the name of a gal who joined some of the mountains boys in the Chattahoochee," said one of the men, scratching his head. He described Robin. "Good shot, too, with the rifle."

"That's *her*." Sturgis said, elated.

"Has a young teen with her," the Revenger said cautiously. "About twelve or thirteen. Your kid?"

Sturgis shook his head. "We don't have any." Then he asked, "*Where* in the Chattahoochee Forest?"

The Revenger proceeded to give descriptions and directions that were meaningless to anyone but a mountain man. Sturgis interrupted him. "How far from here?"

The man pursed his lips and scratched at the grizzle on his chin. " 'Bout two hunnert miles as the crow flies, I'd guess. Don't know if she's still there."

Two hundred miles. So close, yet so far away. Sturgis's heart ached. If he weren't under combat orders now, he would split immediately for the Chattahoochee, and tear the place apart until he found her.

Instead, he wished the Revengers success and moved the C.A.D.S. troops onward. At least Robin was still alive. He would make the rendezvous with her soon. He wondered what the story behind the boy was, and tried to rein in the many thoughts of how Robin might be in danger and need him. He had to complete his mission.

They bivouacked in North Carolina. Sturgis had just taken off his suit and unrolled his bedroll to enjoy a smoke when an explosion shattered the peaceful night air. He ran towards the flash and was greeted by the second horror of the trip: one of his men had been blown to bits inside his suit. Fragments were everywhere, and two other men were injured by shrapnel from the blast. The soldiers who had witnessed it looked stunned.

"What happened?" Sturgis demanded.

"Main power transphasor," one of the eyewitnesses said. "He said he was having trouble with it—the trouble light kept coming on and flickering. He was trying to adjust it . . ."

"*Who* was having trouble?"

"Sergeant Britten, sir."

"Oh, God." Sturgis groaned. Mark Britten—he'd had such high hopes for him. A damn fine fellow and officer, a good soldier right down the line. His life wasted over a wretched equipment failure.

Except this was more than equipment failure—this was *murder*. Those transphasors, along with other faulty parts for the C.A.D.S. suits, had been manufactured by that sleazy outfit, the Exrell Corporation. Sturgis had had the displeasure of meeting up with Exrell's chief executive, Morris "Pinky" Ellis recently. The man was a total scuzzbag, a fat, dirty cretin who delivered cheap, shoddy goods for his lucrative contracts with the government. Pinky had done more for the Reds than one hundred Red generals could have!

Sturgis bent down and picked up pieces of Britten's suit. There wasn't even enough left of the man to bury.

Dr. Sheila de Camp hurried to the scene with her medical satchel. She picked up Britten's twisted name plate, which was lying face down on the ground. When she turned it over and saw the name, Sturgis heard her gasp, then start to cry. To her credit, she quickly stopped her tears and went briskly about her business, tending to two wounded men.

Sturgis clenched his fists at his side. *God damn you to hell forever, Pinky*, he thought. *I will find you again.*

They were deep into Virginia when Sturgis halted the men at the urgent request of Dr. de Camp. While the men relaxed, she took the colonel aside for a private conversation.

"It's radiation sickness, Colonel," she told him. "Two men are too ill to go on—Grigg and Rodriguez."

More bad news. Sturgis was beginning to wonder if the mission were jinxed. "Is it fatal?"

She nodded. "They both tried to cover it up as long as possible. They finally collapsed—literally dropped in their tracks."

"How do you know it's radiation sickness? You told me I had quite a high rad exposure, and I'm not sick."

De Camp shrugged. "Different people have different constitutions, Colonel. Genetic traits might have a lot to do with it. They both have the classic symptoms."

"We'll have to carry them."

"I recommend not moving them. The slightest movement makes them violently ill, and they're losing control over all their bodily functions."

"We can't abandon them like dogs, for crissakes. They're *my men*."

"Can't you leave someone here with them? We could pick them up on the return trip."

Sturgis shot a cold look at de Camp. "Hasn't

anyone told you, Doctor. The odds are we're on a *suicide mission*."

She was shocked. "No—I had no idea—I assumed—"

"Yeah, you assumed. You always assume. You wanted to see the front, de Camp. Well, you've got it in spades. Too late for you to scuttle back to your snug little office in White Sands."

"I have no desire to go back to White Sands, Colonel," she responded, her eyes flashing. "I'm here to do my duty."

"Then do it. Use the Rhino. MacLeish and Rossiter will show you how to set up cots—we've done it before. Just make damn sure those men are out of their misery as much as possible."

Sturgis turned and started walking away. De Camp called after him, "They may not be the only ones, Colonel. I suspect some other men are also suffering from advancing radiation sickness."

Sturgis kept walking and answered over his shoulder. "Then we'll just have to take it as it comes, Doc."

He remounted his tribike and addressed all of the troops over the radio. "We leave in thirty minutes, and we won't stop again until we reach Chesapeake. So far, we've avoided enemy reconnaissance, but we're entering a high-risk zone. Keep your helmets closed and your screens scanning all modes; keep all communication to a minimum."

And pray, he added silently, that our luck holds out.

CHAPTER FOURTEEN

"This is giving me the creeps, Sturge. Something's wrong."

"I don't like it either, Tranh. It's spooky." From the fortieth and top floor of an abandoned office building in Norfolk, Sturgis and Tranh crouched low against the huge windows, surveying the lay of the land before them with the telescopic modes of their suits. The sky boiled with gray-black clouds that showered rain against the window shards. It was a high-rad rain, one that Sturgis knew could fall in torrents for days on end.

They had snuck into the city under the cover of night, they would slip back out again in the coming nightfall. Norfolk itself was a ghost town, patrolled by a few Soviet soldiers, but the nearby U.S. naval base bristled with Reds. It was no wonder the Soviets wanted the Chesapeake Bridge repaired, Sturgis thought—to have easy access to all the abandoned

American military equipment and facilities.

Ahead of them in the mist, at the western edge of the Chesapeake Bay Bridge, slave construction crews labored under the watchful eyes of armed guards. It was easily seen from this vantage point.

"You know what I feel, Sturge? Like the quiet pressure that comes before a tidal wave. It's my intuition."

"Maybe so," Sturgis answered. "You can't stop a tidal wave; we can't stop the mission, either."

Sturgis had halted the Omega Force on the outskirts of Annapolis. He had chosen the southern approach, skirting by night around Raleigh, North Carolina, heading northeast toward Norfolk. It was a good choice, for the Soviets apparently had cleared the freeways of abandoned cars in this part of the country. They had been forced to kill some Russian guards along the way, and tried to make them look like scavenger killings.

But what worried Sturgis and Van Noc now was the absence of any significant resistance on the part of the Russians. Surely soldiers should be more numerous here. They'd had plenty of opportunities to saturate this critical area.

Sturgis ordered "Red mode," then went to "clear screen," normal vision. "It's like they're biding their time, waiting for us. I don't see a trap, but . . ."

"I know," said Tranh. "I've had that feeling of being watched for hours."

"It's got to be Petrin. The other Red generals

usually charge out blasting and try to steam-roller everything in their way. Petrin's crafty."

"And he's got a unit of armor-suited men to be crafty with," Van Noc said.

"At least we haven't seen them here yet. What are the total explosives we're carrying with us, Tranh?"

Van Noc examined the computer readout displayed in his helmet. "We brought two hundred pounds of plastique, type zero-eleven. That should be enough to demolish the entire causeway."

"We've got to rip it end to end," said Sturgis, "—collapse the tunnels and sink the bridge. I want enough wreckage across the channel to close off the upper bay and finish Baltimore as a supply port for the Russians."

"The problem is going to be reaching the bridge," Tranh said. "Red mode estimated five hundred-plus men, concentrated at the main tunnels and causeway. Armed with RPGs and bazookas—approximately one hundred and fifty! I'm also picking up an assortment of howitzer units. And there's an odd heavy mass of metal. Maybe tanks?"

"T-80s," mused Sturgis. "Nuclear-capable with enhanced firepower of 125mm shells and toxic-chemicals canisters. That's their big, forty-two-ton death machine. Are they concentrated or scattered?"

"Concentrated. All at the complex's entrance. It isn't definitely tanks, sir. 'No I.D.' the readout says . . ."

"What about the howitzers? Towed or self-propelled?"

"Towed," responded Van Noc. "Looks like the 122mm babies."

"Good. That gives us more flexibility and them less."

"You know what I'm not getting any reading on?" Tranh said. "Graysuits. How about you?"

"Negative. Those Graysuit bastards have got to be here somewhere. But *where* are they hiding?"

Van Noc went through all the modes of his suit sensors. "Maybe the computer's not separating them out from the machinery around here. I've scanned materials composition, and the answer flashed back negative. They don't seem to be down here. My tie-in with the Rhino doesn't pick any up either."

"I don't believe it. They've found some way to camouflage the Graysuits to avoid detection." He turned stiffly; he'd been in one position nearly all day. A gust of wind slammed a fresh sheet of rain into the building. "The daylight's starting to fade. Let's go. As soon as we get back, assemble the men for the final briefing. Dixon and MacLeish should be back by now." Sturgis had assigned Billy Dixon and Fenton MacLeish to do a reconnaissance to the west—in particular, to check out a Red radar housing on a hill, and to investigate the Red strength at Richmond.

The nuke-age warriors, saving their jetpacks, bounded down the cement stairs, taking a half-dozen at a time. "The slave crews—they're all Americans, aren't they?" Tranh said.

"Mostly. There may be a few Russians who are on somebody's shit list, but I'd wager that ninety-nine percent are Americans."

"There's no way we can save them?"

"None," said Sturgis. "Those are the breaks."

General Petrin was quite pleased with himself. He'd devised a strategy, resisting the impulse to scorch the earth in search of the American Blacksuits before they reached the Chesapeake. Instead, he had decided, *let them come*. The Americans were so few and the Graysuits were so many—the jaws of the Soviet military would close around the Americans like a bear trap, making escape impossible. His troops ought to be able to capture a good number of the Americans, and torture would loosen their tongues about the military strongholds left in the country, and the location of their own base.

Plus, Petrin would at last have a Blacksuit to dissect. He knew the American suit was superior. It was a technology gap he intended to close.

Petrin awaited the Americans at the former U.S. Navy barracks in Norfolk. His temporary quarters were quite comfortable, and he had plenty of good, rad-free food.

He was relieved when suddenly the *Lenin* was ordered to Charleston by the Kremlin. Petrin was confident he didn't need the *Lenin*, and he certainly could do without Veloshnikov breathing down his neck.

He had made elaborate preparations for engaging the Americans. He had installed one hundred ninety Spetsnaz Graysuits in a revamped building on the grounds, which was protected by an antiradar shield. He had gotten special shields for his bazooka teams, to protect them from armor-piercing shells. He had positioned the bazookas, howitzers, and tanks along the western freeway approach to the bridge. At the Richmond airport, he had on standby alert six Sukhoi-24 all-weather attack jets, each armed to the max with 8,000 kilograms of firepower, including 30mm cannons and AS-7 air-to-surface missiles. The Sukhoi-24 was especially suited to high-speed, low-level action. They would augment his Graysuits.

He purposefully had not stationed the Sukhois in Norfolk, where the Blacksuits would be likely to see them. Richmond was not far away, and the Sukhois would cover the distance in minutes.

Petrin saw the upcoming battle as a classic encounter. He would meet the American vanguard head-on at the blocked western terminus of the bridge. His troops would execute a flanking maneuver and, backed by an overwhelming artillery barrage, drive straight into the enemy for a point-blank firefight. It would be fast and dirty. Petrin excelled at this tactic, so much so that no recovery plan existed in case of defeat. There would be *no* defeat.

Petrin smiled as Kurchiev came in with a bottle of

Stolichnaya vodka and two glasses. Just the thing!

"Men, we're going to have one hell of a gauntlet to run. You've heard the reports." Sturgis slapped the crude map hung behind him. He had drawn the map on packing paper found in the abandoned Quickie Mart convenience store in the community of Little Creek, outside of Norfolk, where his squad had taken refuge against being spotted. The store was stripped of all its edible and usable goods and had a hollow, lonely feeling. Rain pounded on the windows and roof.

"You know the setup. There may be air fire, Sukhois, or MIGs. Keep a sky-scan. I expect Graysuits, though I don't know exactly where and when. I'm gratified we're within two miles of target without being spotted. It's a real break if it's true. We'll do a max-speed assault from here. No more hiding or sneaking—it won't work."

Sturgis brandished the blue felt marker, which he had found in the Quickie Mart's storeroom, and began drawing circles, *x*'s and arrows. He had a lit cigarette butt clamped in his lips. His adrenaline was up, as it always was in anticipation of a fight. He sensed the same high-voltage charge among his men, a long-odds, do-or-die determination that put everyone on a razor edge. He felt taut inside, almost high; his thoughts raced.

"The Rhino's going to be here on the west, shooting down Sukhois or anything else the Reds fly out. We're going to push the tribikes to maximum speed, as fast as we can take this wet pavement, and drive straight down 301. Teams A, B, and C—that's me, Dixon, and Van Noc—will continue to the new entrance tunnel to the whole, long complex. To do that, we have to go straight down the last leg of the interstate, right past the Reds. The other squads will split about here"—he jabbed at the map—"into flanking maneuvers to the right and left along the service roads.

"A, B, and C are direct-assault teams and will lay the plastique at the assigned spots, which I will detonate. Eight out of ten of our tribikes carry explosives. If I fall, if I get taken out, MacLeish will detonate from the Rhino. Once the charges are laid, we all get to the areas designated at the outskirts of Norfolk.

"This is going to be a last mission for a lot of us, but we've got a good chance of succeeding in the objective if we give it everything we've got at all costs. As usual, men, if you're taken prisoner, you must self-destruct."

"What about any Americans out there working on the bridge, Colonel?" one of the new recruits asked.

The colonel shook his head. "Son, you're going to have to forget they're Americans—for the sake of *all* Americans."

Sturgis spent the next hour reviewing details of the attack plan and evasive maneuvers, and answering questions. He denied Dr. Sheila de Camp's petition to ride in the frontal attack. "You'll be in the Rhino," he said. "You'll have more than enough to do when it's all over."

At last Sturgis looked at his watch and ended the briefing. "Okay, we've got ten minutes. Then we get this hellshow on the road. Get to your bikes!"

At a hundred and twenty miles per hour into the wind, the rain hit the C.A.D.S. suits like little bullets, pinging and tearing away in the slipstreams created by the racing tribikes. The entire world looked steel-gray: the heavy layer of storm clouds, the landscape that rushed by in a blur, the ribbon of asphalt beneath them. Sturgis was hunched over his bike with a tight grip on the bars. He had filtered out the shriek of the engines to listen for other noises. He was barreling toward the target, straight down the interstate, past startled Soviet tank crews.

A readout warned him of enemy fire, coming at them from eleven and one o'clock. The Probability of Destruction estimate was .0015. The suit's computer said the rockets would pass over him and strike behind. He wasn't too worried about the men to the rear. C.A.D.S. suits were virtually impervious to anything but a square-on hit. A near-miss might blast a trooper off a bike, but the man should be able to get up and right his bike.

The shells streaked by Sturgis and hit in the rear of

the formation, where computer control swerved a man's tribike deftly to clear the blasts and shock waves. More rockets came at them, from all angles. Shouts sounded over the radio as several men were hurled from their bikes.

One man was thrown high into the air from the impact, and came down to the hard ground with a sickening crash. His suit saved his life, but the mechanisms were destroyed, and he lay on his back like a helpless insect, unable to get up or see out his cracked visor.

He struggled in a daze to right himself, then suddenly saw blurry forms appear around him and men bending down to try to lift him up. At first he thought they were his buddies, then realized the suit figures were wrong. They were black, but they were *different*! He activated the self-destruct, and the yellow fireball of an explosion took six Russian Graysuits painted black, with him into death's domain.

General Petrin, watching the action from a vantage point closer to the terminus of the bridge, was quick to see the ineffectiveness of the bazookas, He ordered out the big tanks into action. A barricade across the highway was dropped in front of the Americans—and another a mile behind.

"Good," Petrin muttered. "The trap closes."

The 122mm tank shells succeeded where the bazooka had failed, tearing apart Blacksuits on the road. The rear of the C.A.D.S. column, led by Roberto Fuentes, slowed and split into flanks and began diverting the heavy artillery by returning fire. E-balls sizzled through the air. Visibility was virtually nil due to rain, and the smoke, dirt, and debris kicked up by all the shelling, and the Americans had to use their special screen modes for their bearings. They succeeded in blowing several tanks to smithereens.

A tank shell exploded in front of Fuentes and the man beside him, throwing them off their feet. Fuentes jetted up and, in a brief clearing of the air, saw that his companion was also up, sending off E-balls through his right-arm weapons system. With a shock, Roberto saw the man's left arm was missing—the shell blast had taken it clean off at the shoulder. The man suddenly fell to the ground.

Fuentes locked on to the tank and fired an E-ball. It made contact and the tank was blown into fragments.

Up ahead, Sturgis's computer readings flashed a warning at him as a tank lumbered into his path. TEN SECONDS TO IMPACT, the readout told him. PROBABILITY OF DESTRUCTION .9555. Instantly Sturgis released his bike and activated his jets. He soared in a bounding leap up over the tank as the bike smashed into it and was crushed beneath the treads. He came down swiftly on the opposite side, whirled, and fired two E-balls just as the tank's gun turrets were rotating toward him. The tank exploded, knocking him off his feet.

Around him, other members of the lead teams had done the same fast thinking, losing their tribikes but saving themselves with their suits intact. They were up against a huge barrier of thick steel. Sturgis fired two E-balls, but they failed to more than dent the barrier. At the same time, the Russian tanks were busy blasting his men. Damn!

Sturgis was aware of the toll being taken on his men. The shelling was accentuated by the cries of dying. *"Mode red!"* he yelled. The locations of everyone in the unit were displayed on his visor as blue dots. Sturgis leapt into the air on his jets and saw that the huge road barrier actually fitted flush against the tunnel entrance ahead. He fired three E-balls at it without effect. They were trapped.

Suddenly the Graysuits charged out from hidden bunkers, coming at the Americans in long, leaping strides.

Billy Dixon was occupied with a howitzer in front of him when he was seized from the rear by one of the Russian special-forces men. Though the American suit was technologically superior to the Russian version, the suits were equally matched in servo-strength, and the two men wrestled in a hand-to-hand fight, the Russian attempting to smash the visor on the American's suit. With a flick, a steel spike appeared on the Russian's wrist, and he jabbed at Billy, aiming for vulnerable joints. They swung and shoved at each other like mighty Goliaths.

Billy managed to shoot off some rounds of machine-gun bullets and darts, but they bounded harmlessly off the Graysuits the same as they did off a C.A.D.S. suit. Billy switched to E-balls, figuring to destroy them both. But his magazine was empty. He braced himself for the Russian version of electro-ball fire, but none came. Either the Russian was out also, or he had no comparable weapons. In any case, the enemy was bent on getting him with the spike. Billy dodged and parried. His radio antenna bent, nearly cutting his communication, but he wasn't about to call for help anyway—every soldier had his hands full trying to stay alive.

But his jetpacks still worked, and Billy burned the jets for a short lift, intending to kick the Russian in the face and jump over him. He lashed out and the Russian snapped back, but caught Dixon's leg as he went over the man's head. He crashed to the ground and they rolled over and over each other. The Russian stabbed wildly with his blade and swiftly found his mark in one of the vulnerable joints between Billy's neck and shoulder. The American's electrocircuits began to short. Punching wildly, Billy managed to crush the Russian's faceplate into his face, and then he fell.

Back in the Rhino, Rossiter and MacLeish reacted quickly when the radar showed blips coming over the horizon from the northwest. "Sukhois," said Rossiter. "Half a dozen, bearing ten o'clock."

"Coming in low and fast," said MacLeish. The

Rhino's computer zeroed in on the lead jet, and MacLeish fired a surface-to-air missile. Within moments, the computer screen registered a contact and the blip vanished. The remaining Sukhois reacted instantly, splitting formation. Two kept heading straight for the tunnel while the other three banked and came for the Rhino.

"This is going to be interesting," grimaced Rossiter. The Rhino's computer was already reacting to the trajectories of the missiles coming from the Sukhois, its big gun turrets spinning to return fire to explode them in the air. The guns couldn't move fast enough to catch the missiles from all three jets, and the Rhino rocked as rockets exploded around them on the ground. "Hang on, Doc," Rossiter shouted, twisting the battlewagon sideways in evasive maneuvering.

"Get me to the wounded!" de Camp yelled.

"Sorry, Doc, it'll have to wait till we take care of these babies," Rossiter said between clenched teeth.

MacLeish crawled topside and manually maneuvered the Rhino's twin machine guns. Cannons firing, the Sukhois strafed the Rhinos. The bullets chewed into the metal with deafening noise. A burst of accurate fire from MacLeish caught one of the Sukhois at a fuel tank attached to one of the wing glove pylons. Fuel streamed out and ignited in an inferno—but inside the Rhino, all the angry doc saw was another radar blip disappearing from the screen.

They took out another Russian jet with a Redeye missile, then homed in on the last fighter. A missile from the Sukhoi caught the Rhino with a deflecting hit and blew a hole in a wheel. The engines stalled and clanked to a halt. "Sitting ducks now," said Rossiter, trying to restart the engines.

Just as the Sukhoi was banking for another strafe, MacLeish fired the last Redeye missile. "Contact!" he shouted. An abrupt silence fell over the Rhino.

Sturgis had retrieved two explosive packs from his tribike. Resourceful Tranh and Fuentes also grabbed their packages of death.

Sturgis had to find a way to get into their target, and they were outnumbered at least two to one by the Graysuits. The Russian trap was good, and the only thing that was keeping the Americans from being obliterated was the superiority of their suits. Thank God for American technology, Sturgis thought, as he sent an E-ball into the midriff of a Graysuit. The man disintegrated into fragments. Tracers lit up the scene in strobes of light.

Sturgis had located Roberto and Tranh, who were not far away. "We've got to blow this barricade," he said. "Quick, bring me *all* your plastique. I'll put it with mine and stick it on the barrier. On my signal, fire your E-balls *with me*. Maybe the E-balls *plus* the charges can budge it."

Sturgis, Roberto, and Tranh jammed their explosives against the barricade and then jetted away, under a hail of RPG fire. The ground was pitted with blast holes, and was an obstacle course of debris and wounded men. The explosion probably would kill some C.A.D.S. men, but it had to be done!

They came down and took refuge behind a smashed truck about one thousand feet from the barricade. Sturgis yelled, "Link suits' Fire Controls . . . Fire!" The three fired their E-balls at the planted charges simultaneously.

With a mighty roar, the huge steel barricade blew up into the air in two giant pieces. The tunnel was open!

Rossiter, keeping one eye on the long-range radar, roared the spherical-wheeled battlewagon down the road toward Sturgis and his men. Fenton, who was topside, saw the explosion rip open the tunnel entrance and muttered, "Thank God." Now the mission had its chance. He began manually directing the vehicle's twin guns at approaching Soviet bazooka squads. Rossiter yelled, "Fenton, there are T-80 tanks, loaded for bear, heading out of an opening garage shutter a hundred meters away, bearing two thirty degrees—Use the missiles!"

Rossiter got into the missile control seat, spun the array of death around. He laser-tagged the tanks. A Redeye missile shot from the rack atop the battlewagon, the exhaust flames passing harmlessly over Rossiter's C.A.D.S. suit. The tanks erupted in cherry-red balls of metal and flesh. "Tanks for the memories," Rossiter chuckled.

Sturgis saw the Rhino coming through the smoke

and fire. "Hurry, Rossiter! *Come on!* Get in the tunnel with us . . ."

There was a brief silence—Fenton and Rossiter were speaking to each other on an inside-vehicle communications channel. Then Fenton spoke: "Negative, Commander. The Rhino's too slow. Don't wait for us. You need me to guard your rear. A whole mess of PV-7 pursuit vehicles with racks of Zircon-2 missiles just came on our distance radar. You go on, finish the mission. We don't want to burn out the drive shaft trying to keep up with you speed demons. So long, Colonel. It's been swell. Over and out."

Sturgis tried, but neither Fenton nor Rossiter answered his radio calls. And time was wasting. "Goodbye, you damned heroes, I'll miss ya both," he said. And he meant it.

CHAPTER FIFTEEN

Sturgis rallied his remaining men. Now that he had blasted open the tunnel entrance, it was time to formulate a new plan of attack. How could he maximize the effect of the remaining Commandos?

In a few seconds he came up with a plan. Maybe it wasn't the best plan, but he had to think on his feet. It would have to do. "Men," he shouted. "Retrieve the satchel explosives from your fallen comrades' tribikes. Then follow me—through the breach."

His men hurried around, all the while taking heavy incoming fire from Graysuits, returning fire. They rushed from one overturned tribike to another, doing as ordered. Sturgis did likewise. Soon he had scooped up five more packages of the deadly 0-11 explosives from the grisly death scenes. There was no time to stop and see if any of the bloodied Blacksuits contained living souls. The enemy wouldn't be seizing lots of damaged suits, though. Sturgis knew the booby-trap-rigged combat gear would blast whole bunches of Red experts to hell if they tried to pry them open without the correct disassembly codes.

He got on his tribike. A stream of submachine-gun fire pinged off his helmet. He swung around and made target acquisition—a Graysuit running down an incline. Sturgis lifted his right arm and leveled it at the Russian. "Fire E-ball," he ordered. Instantly the high-velocity semiliquid electrostatically charged shell shot from his arm mount and slashed through the Red's combat suit like a hot knife through butter.

Sturgis roared his bike to life and, wheels spinning, tore into the darkness of the tunnel.

Just outside of Charleston, South Carolina, in the brocaded upper bedroom of his Tara mansion, Veloshnikov slammed down the phone receiver. "Damn!" He tried to calm himself looking out the French windows at the newly green weeping willows swaying in the breeze. Sturgis had broken through into the tunnel. He and his Tech Commandos—the infamous Blacksuits—were destroying his U.S. occupation plan. There was no way he could control his emotions over *that*.

Petrin! Petrin had *again* promised to vanquish the Blacksuits and again had *not* delivered! Veloshnikov turned to his reflection in the tall gilt-edged mirror. He wasn't surprised to see his whole face reddened. The vein over his right eye was standing out. High blood pressure! The supreme marshal was beside himself with rage. He picked up the cordless phone receiver and threw it at the mirror, which shattered. "Petrin will pay with his life if my great plan is destroyed!"

As Sturgis zoomed into the tunnel, his strobes automatically flickered at maximum intensity to light the way. He swerved around several turns in the long, tiled highway tunnel. Gathering speed, the big barrel tires squealed, sending out a trail of sparks and smoke behind him. At least a score of tribikes driven by the surviving C.A.D.S. members roared and whined in his wake. Switching to Red mode, Sturgis asked the computer, "How many men left?" The red number 38 lit up and moved across the lower part of his visor.

Thirty-eight would have to be enough. Assuming each man behind him had five packages in his possession, Sturgis told the computer to come up with a distance-between-charges figure for the twenty-mile-long complex.

Instantly the calculation was made based on an analysis of the facility stored in the suit's memory chips. THROW CHARGES EVERY 300 METERS, the read-out concluded.

Sturgis hoped to hell that was right—the suit and its built-in computer had taken a beating. If it slipped a digit, it could foul up the whole operation.

This was it. If those plastic-explosive satchels didn't stick to the concrete and tile walls of the tunnel . . .

They would, "Men," he told the unit over the commlink, "I want an explosive package every three hundred meters all along this twenty-mile stretch. Form a single line. First man throws his load first, then the next man—all on your left, if possible—so the others can spot them. Throw them so they stick at about eye level."

Sturgis grimaced. They'd lost so many men that the original plan, assigning each man to specific areas, was null and void. They'd have to wing it.

"See you all on the other side, in Cape Charles at Area A," he concluded.

Sturgis threw the first of his packages deftly at a support beam, a smooth section of concrete. It stuck like it was a fly in a spider's web. He couldn't help exclaiming, "It works!"

He was doing a hundred and ten miles per hour on the straight and smooth surface, hugging the centerline. It was all he could do to maintain control of the vehicle and still throw accurately. At the fifth throw, the package didn't stick. But the man behind him—Roberto, by the sound of his Spanish curse words when he saw what happened—threw his first package to fill the gap—and it stuck.

Sturgis increased speed to a hundred and thirty miles per hour. In a few seconds, he roared out of the tunnel onto a long white concrete causeway dazzling in the noonday sun. All around him the quiet Chesapeake waters stretched to the horizon. It was a beautiful day—all of a sudden. The first clear blue sky he'd seen since the twenty-minute war last Christmas Eve.

The helmet visor compensated for the glare automatically, sensing his squint. "Air scan—G.I. mode," he ordered.

The suit computer adjusted his screen to penetrate a twelve- to fifty-mile radius. The readout crossed the bottom of his visorscreen, NO AIRCRAFT.

Give them time, he thought grimly. They'll be here as soon as they realize their ground trap didn't stop us.

According to Jerry Jeff Jeeters's, Bible code messages, the whole Chesapeake Bridge tunnel complex was now completed after being repaired and rebuilt. Special alterations had been made to both widen and strengthen the complex to take the large Soviet tanks. Sturgis knew he'd have to be on the alert for these changes. The roadway might be very different from the information contained on the Rhino's pre-reconstruction maps.

Sturgis heard a beep in his ear. On Forward scan, the Radar mode clicked on and a warning came on the readout before the colonel's eyes. BARRIER—WOODEN—1300 METERS.

Sturgis hit the brakes, slowing to fifty miles per hour abruptly. The barrier was just inside the dark entrance to the next tunnel. The clever bastards thought they would waste any enemy speeding unseeing into the darkness. But the C.A.D.S. suits had supernormal abilities, and were capable of infinite variations on the theme of *destruction*. He'd make short work of the barrier. "Interface targeting with tribike," he said calmly. He heard a click. "Lock Hawk missile on barrier of wood."

LOCKED, came the readout.

"Fire!"

One of the tribike's missiles roared out in front of Sturgis, keeping a few feet off the pavement, at thousands of feet per second.

For an instant he was lost in the exhaust smoke, which would have burned him had he not been in the suit. Then the smoke blew away, just as the target was hit. Pieces of wood spun up and out of the tunnel entrance. The suit-computer readout indicated that the obstruction to the continued passage of the Americans was eliminated—but what was next, inside the tunnel?

Sturgis roared into the darkness once again. Roberto yelled out, "Got my explosives stuck all along the causeway we just passed, Commander. Tranh is next; he'll make sure this tunnel is wasted."

"Good." Sturgis wiped the dust from the barrier's explosion off his visor.

Then he accessed Red mode, which showed the position of each surviving member of the team, and counted the long string of riders—thirty-eight. All surviving members of the C.A.D.S. team were accounted for.

Suddenly there were thirty-nine. The thirty-ninth blip displayed at the top of his screen was dark green—an enemy vehicle. G.I. mode identified it as a Soviet-designed pursuit vehicle—supercharged and racked with missile launchers. The blinking green dot turned to red—meaning pursuer. Sturgis accessed T.A. mode, anticipating the firing of a missile from the Soviet vehicle. It fired. The trajectory analysis flashed across Sturgis's visorscreen.

The rearmost of Sturgis's men suddenly vanished from the display. Then another man. The pursuer was knocking off the few men the Tech Commando had left.

"Last man," Sturgis yelled. "Drop your satchel charges behind you. Set for five seconds."

Billy had been too busy keeping his fuel-leaking tribike up with the others—his steering was a bit off, too—and so he'd failed to scan behind him and see Arlen and Joyner die. But Dixon's response now rang out. "I'm setting my charges, sir. Five seconds?"

"Right!" Sturgis yelled. "Expedite!"

Billy hefted the charges off his bike and increased speed to a wheel-wobbling one hundred m.p.h, leaning low. His probability-of-destruct analysis said he was being targeted. .9017.

Major Penshov had seen the packs fly from the strange American motorcycle he was pursuing. He couldn't stop fast enough. Too late, he hit the brakes. Smoke poured from the brake calipers gripping the four wheels on each axle. The packages had stuck to the smooth walls of the tunnel. He'd never seen an object that size just *stick* on smooth concrete like that! What was it?—*a bomb*. It had to be *a bomb*.

The delay in Penshov's recognition was fatal. He was right up alongside the bombs now. He could see them—mines of some sort—knubbed edges, a time meter . . . He let up on the brakes; the only chance now was to pass it before it exploded. He roared the missile car forward, his head slamming back against the foam neck support of his seat.

The world suddenly grew orange. The car was spinning end over end, shooting down the tunnel, skimming the road surface. The bombs had gone off just behind him. The hood and windshield now grated along the surface of the road. And the major was held upside down by his harness. Sparks, red-hot metal, and broken glass assaulted his face. He tried to shield himself with his hands. The huge armored pursuit vehicle was upside down, but he was alive. He wasn't seriously hurt! He smiled.

But not for long. For a huge tidal wave of bay water was coming from the ruptured side of the tunnel where the explosives had gone off. Suddenly he was underwater, struggling, fighting, with bloody hands stuck with glass fragments, to get the jammed harness seat belt off. He held his breath as long as he could. But then Penshov had to breathe—and there was only water in the tunnel.

Dixon had been nearly thrown from the tribike by the concussions behind him. But the tunnel bent slightly at this point, partly shielding him from the explosions. The Russian pursuit vehicle had been hit, destroyed. But now there was another danger. Billy could only get his bike up to a hundred miles per hour, and the wall of surging, frothy water bursting through the ruptured tunnel walls, powered by the enormous pressure of the bay waters, was pursuing him. "Colonel," he yelled out, "I'm not so sure . . ."

Sturgis watched the red dot slip closer and closer on his visor grid display to the green line following it—the wall of water. But there was a white grid line just ahead of Billy.

With relief Sturgis yelled, "You're coming to the exit of the tunnel, Billy. You'll be on the causeway in twenty-one seconds. Hang in there. Fire your rear missile to gain speed."

"Good idea, Skip," Billy yelled. His bike picked up speed as he fired the missile. Nevertheless, the wall of water was just a few feet behind him when he roared into the next patch of daylight. He was on the second stretch of causeway, supported by a low-lying island that was probably submerged at high tide. The water subsided, sought its own level. Billy had made it.

From an altitude of one thousand feet, General Petrin circled over the bridge complex in his Ilyushin reconnaissance jet. The American Blacksuits had broken through. He'd never have thought they could make it, but they did. They were now streamed out on the long causeway below him, throwing packages of what he presumed were time-delay explosives. Probably the mile-long tunnel behind them had been littered with similar devices before it blew. The general frowned and ordered the pilot, his aide Kurchiev, to bank the small radar-concealed jet. His instruments indicated the Sukhoi attack jets were still miles away. It would be minutes until they arrived—they might come too late.

But he had one thin hope. Veloshnikov had insisted that captive American men and women—even children—be brought to the Chesapeake. Now—by Veloshnikov's orders—thousands were chained on the causeway bridge of the Chesapeake complex.

Hostages! The Americans wouldn't blow up their own people. They hadn't in the past. They wouldn't now. The American commander would try to free them, get them off the long causeway—wasting precious minutes. By then the Sukhoi jets would have arrived; the special pursuit cars would have caught up with the incredibly speedy three-wheeled motorcycles the Blacksuits drove.

Yes, *hostages*. That would stop them. The soft-hearted Americans would sacrifice their objective to save the hostages. They were always "Mr. Nice Guy." That's why they finished last . . .

Sturgis saw that they were coming to a major span now. The big girders had been recently painted a new coat of Soviet red. He roared past a toll notice, increasing speed as the asphalt below him widened. Sturgis now saw the chained men and women—U.S. hostages—over a thousand of them secured about their waists, spaced every fifty yards or so along both sides of the bridge. They had seen the fire and smoke of the tunnel explosions and the tidal wave that followed. They knew they were about to die. Their only chance of saving themselves was for the Commandos to stop and free them. But they *didn't want* to be freed! They waved Sturgis on. All along the road behind him, the C.A.D.S. men tossed their surprise packages for the Reds against the girders of the bridge. Yet, as Sturgis zoomed along he heard, "Way to go! Way to go!" shouted over and over in a chant.

The hostages knew it meant their own lives! And still they yelled, "Don't stop. Don't stop for us!"

Sturgis knew this was the last stretch. Would the bombs last, though?

"Who's in front of Billy?" Sturgis yelled.

"Guess that's me," Parker said. "He can't keep up,

Colonel. Do you think I should slow down and—"

"No. That's orders, Parker. No man can jeopardize the success of the mission. Keep maximum speed . . . Did you throw your packages yet?"

"Yup—on the bridge. I guess that's the last of them. We won't get to blow this last causeway area—but, we did pretty good."

Sturgis agreed. He looked forward and ordered, "Telescopic mode, ten-power." Immediately the Cape Charles coast—at the end of the causeway—sprung closer. The way was clear.

"Scan for aircraft," Sturgis ordered the computer. There was a beeper warning. Twelve miles above them and dropping fast—six Sukhoi jets.

"Plot aircraft—C.A.D.S. intercept time."

ONE MINUTE 32 SECONDS. Enough time to make the shore—for all except Billy.

Sturgis set the last of his tribike missiles to fire when a jet came in range, hoping the small Stinger missile would lock onto and devastate the attack jet.

The six attack jets now appeared on Petrin's radar. He smiled. He'd command them from here, wheel around, watch them strafe and pick off the Blacksuits while the Americans stopped for the hostages.

The plane banked so that he could see the causeway. *What?* The Americans whizzed by their friends. The slave workers chained along the route were waving their hands, encouraging them not to stop, but to speed on. Great Lenin! They weren't stopping!

Sturgis was off the causeway now, roaring down a highway leading to Norfolk. Knowing the jets were near, he tore forward at maximum speed—a hundred and sixty miles per hour. He headed off a ramp toward Area A, a parking garage located under a small office building. He was relieved to find it there. It could have been destroyed, after all, even if Cape Charles hadn't been hit by a Soviet nuke. But it was there—and it was good cover.

An E-ball took care of the entrance barrier that demanded to see his "Mall Parking Permit."

The large underground concrete garage was like a bunker. It should hold, unless the jets got a shot right into the entrance . . .

The other tribikes roared in behind him. His readouts indicated that Billy was still on the causeway, but a mile from shore. The jets were coming in at just above the water, heading toward Cape Charles. One jet had peeled off and was heading toward Billy.

Sturgis had no choice. He read off the computer code that would ignite by radio the string of sixty-seven explosives they had left behind. His father's birthdate. That was so he wouldn't forget the numbers that activated the explosives: 12–31–33!

Petrin watched all but one tribike leave the causeway. That last Blacksuit vehicle seemed to have a mechanical problem, judging from the smoke. Petrin knew the Americans would not wait for him.

Petrin knew what was about to happen. Something, that to his knowledge, the Americans had never done before. They were going to blow up *their own people*. And soon. "Quickly," he shouted to Kurchiev, "*Climb*. *Climb* at maximum velocity. There is going to be a terrible explosion! Climb, you fool. Climb!"

Petrin's small jet had climbed to 6540 meters when it happened. Peering anxiously through his high power binoculars against the cockpit's side window, Petrin saw the long line—twenty miles of concrete and steel silhouetted against the blue waters below. Suddenly it turned orange and red in dozens of evenly spaced places. My God, they were powerful explosives! The waters shot up in the intense, blackish, jagged smoke clouds that spelled the end of the Red master plan.

Tidal waves resulting from the concussions moved out in circles from a hundred spots along the collapsing line of road below him. Shock waves traveling upward caused heavy turbulence, tossing and pitching the small jet as if it were a rowboat in the ocean. Petrin's binoculars slammed against the cockpit's window, hurting the bridge of his nose. "Steady this thing, idiot," he screamed at Kurchiev, who was doing his best to regain control of the jet.

As the smoke cleared, the damage could be plainly seen. The girders were twisted and bent as if by a giant hand. The causeway was gone in most places. For a moment it had just hung in thin air—and then, sagging under its own weight, had fallen and splashed into the roiling waters.

"General," gasped Kurchiev. "They did it. They blew it up . . ."

"Yes," Petrin sighed, putting down his binoculars. "They did it even though the hostages were on it. The

Americans aren't being 'Mr. Nice Guy' anymore . . ."

In the garage, Sturgis and his men could hear the distant explosions resound like a series of immense cannons firing in close sequence. Though the charges had all gone off simultaneously, they'd been strung out for twenty miles, making the sounds take different lengths of time to reach them. Sturgis smiled. "Mission accomplished," he said. They all threw up their arms and cheered.

The building shook with the tremendous impact of the shock waves from Soviet air-to-ground missiles. Several hits, from the sound of it. The roar and whine of the supersonic attack jets filled his Audiomode. Sturgis and his men dismounted their bikes. "Men," he said as they formed up, "you all know the plan. If we hadn't been spotted coming in here, it would have been different. But we were. So now *scatter* through the area, each man heading in a different direction. Then enter the water. Stay under, and keep spread out. Walk on the bottom over to gridpoint W on the Virginia shore. It's about six point seven miles. The coordinates are locked on your computers. Just follow its guidance.

"Thanks to your bravery, the unit has achieved its objective. Now we've got to get the hell out of here." He paused. "Any questions?"

"Sir," said one of the men in the forward ranks. "My suit has some holes."

Sturgis said, "I'm sorry, soldier, very sorry. You know what you must do."

"Yessir." He snapped to attention, saluting. "Orders are to abandon and destroy suit and try to escape on foot up the coast—"

"Countermand the order, Lieutenant Grimes. That suit ain't worth shit compared to an experienced Tech Commando's ability to take on the enemy. I have a job for you. A dangerous one. Five minutes after we get out of here, I want you to take your tribike and get on the highway headed north. Have the other tribikes follow you on autopilot—guided by you. Get it?"

The voice was steady and resolute now. "*Yessir*. I am to persuade the enemy that I am *the entire force*—a decoy ploy."

"Can you do it?"

"Yessir; thank you, sir."

"Good luck, Grimes. One more thing," Sturgis said, as another concussion shook the building above, sending chunks of concrete down to their left, "—Don't let the Reds get their hands on the tribikes. If it looks as if you're going to be caught, overload the tribikes' power packs. That should blow them up in a matter of minutes, leaving only twisted scrap metal for the Reds to analyze—if that. The few minutes should give you time enough to get away . . ."

Turning to the rest of the men, Sturgis ordered, "Let's go!" The men began jogging to the many exits out of the building, rushing across the streets, taking cover in other buildings. In a matter of minutes they were scattered over a half-mile radius. The tremendous power of the C.A.D.S. suits allowed them to smash through walls between buildings—further complicating the task of the airmen above to destroy them.

Lieutenant Grimes had a last cigarette while he waited the five minutes alone. Then he spat it out, slammed his visor down, mounted his tribike—and locked the other tribikes' navigation systems to his suit computer. He was just about to roar out into the outside world, when he heard a whine.

The dusty, scorched tribike and its Blacksuited rider slid in alongside Grimes. The visor came up. It was *Billy*.

"The jet didn't get me. *I* got the jet," he said proudly. "And I've been listening to you all talking. You take the front of the tribike column; I'll control the rear. It'll be easier that way. Let's go!"

"Boy! You are something else, Dixon," Grimes said. "Glad to see you're still alive!"

"Rebels never die," Billy said.

Deep under the swiftly flowing water of the bay halfway across to the Virginia shore, thirty meters deep and unobserved, Sturgis and his men—the twenty-six that had made it—were spread out walking on the bottom. It was a slow, hard walk in the heavy suits, but they would make it at least to the shore. What would be waiting for them when they came out of the water on the other side, he didn't know—maybe nothing. Maybe *death*. If so, they would die as victors, not as the vanquished. The Red plan for U.S. domination had been dealt a serious blow. He'd never been so proud of his fellow freedom fighters as at this moment.

In the utter silence of the dark waters, he moved forward, toward whatever fate awaited him.

THE ZONE
by James Rouch

Across the hellish strip of Western Europe known as The Zone, super tanks armed with tactical nuclear weapons, lethal chemicals, and fiercely accurate missiles roam the germ-infested terrain. War in the mist-enshrouded Zone is a giant game of hide and seek—with a deadly booby prize for the losers.

#1: HARD TARGET	(1492, $2.50)
#2: BLIND FIRE	(1588, $2.50)
#3: HUNTER KILLER	(1662, $2.50)
#4: SKY STRIKE	(1770, $2.50)
#5: OVERKILL	(1832, $2.50)

Available wherever paperbacks are sold, or order direct from the Publisher. Send cover price plus 50¢ per copy for mailing and handling to Zebra Books, Dept. 1893, 475 Park Avenue South, New York, N.Y. 10016. Residents of New York, New Jersey and Pennsylvania must include sales tax. DO NOT SEND CASH.

THE SURVIVALIST SERIES
by Jerry Ahern

#1: TOTAL WAR	(0960, $2.50)
#2: THE NIGHTMARE BEGINS	(0810, $2.50)
#3: THE QUEST	(0851, $2.50)
#4: THE DOOMSAYER	(0893, $2.50)
#5: THE WEB	(1145, $2.50)
#6: THE SAVAGE HORDE	(1232, $2.50)
#7: THE PROPHET	(1339, $2.50)
#8: THE END IS COMING	(1374, $2.50)
#9: EARTH FIRE	(1405, $2.50)
#10: THE AWAKENING	(1478, $2.50)
#11: THE REPRISAL	(1590, $2.50)
#12: THE REBELLION	(1676, $2.50)

Available wherever paperbacks are sold, or order direct from the Publisher. Send cover price plus 50¢ per copy for mailing and handling to Zebra Books, Dept. 1893, 475 Park Avenue South, New York, N.Y. 10016. Residents of New York, New Jersey and Pennsylvania must include sales tax. DO NOT SEND CASH.

THE WARLORD SERIES
by Jason Frost

THE WARLORD (1189, $3.50)
A series of natural disasters, starting with an earthquake and leading to nuclear power plant explosions, isolates California. Now, cut off from any help, the survivors face a world in which law is a memory and violence is the rule.

Only one man is fit to lead the people, a man raised among Indians and trained by the Marines. He is Erik Ravensmith, The Warlord—a deadly adversary and a hero for our times.

#2: THE CUTTHROAT (1308, $2.50)

#3: BADLAND (1437, $2.50)

#4: PRISONLAND (1506, $2.50)

#5: TERMINAL ISLAND (1697, $2.50)

Available wherever paperbacks are sold, or order direct from the Publisher. Send cover price plus 50¢ per copy for mailing and handling to Zebra Books, Dept. 1893, 475 Park Avenue South, New York, N.Y. 10016. Residents of New York, New Jersey and Pennsylvania must include sales tax. DO NOT SEND CASH.

SAIGON COMMANDOS
by Jonathan Cain

It is Vietnam as we've never seen it before, revealed with bitter reality and love – of a people and a place.

SAIGON COMMANDOS	(1283, $3.25)
#2: CODE ZERO: SHOTS FIRED!	(1329, $2.50)
#4: CHERRY-BOY BODY BAG	(1407, $2.50)
#5: BOONIE-RAT BODY BURNING	(1441, $2.50)
#6: DI DI MAU OR DIE	(1493, $2.50)
#7: SAC MAU, VICTOR CHARLIE	(1574, $2.50)
#8: YOU DIE, DU MA!	(1629, $2.50)
#9: MAD MINUTE	(1698, $2.50)
#10: TORTURERS OF TET	(1772, $2.50)
#11: HOLLOWPOINT HELL	(1848, $2.50)
#12: SUICIDE SQUAD	(1897, $2.50)

Available wherever paperbacks are sold, or order direct from the Publisher. Send cover price plus 50¢ per copy for mailing and handling to Zebra Books, Dept. 1893, 475 Park Avenue South, New York, N.Y. 10016. Residents of New York, New Jersey and Pennsylvania must include sales tax. DO NOT SEND CASH.